yeti boy

Also by Kara May

The Dream Snatcher

First published in Great Britain in hardback by Collins in 1999
This edition published in paperback in 2000
Collins is an imprint of HarperCollins*Publishers* Ltd
77-85 Fulham Palace Road, Hammersmith, London W6 8JB

The HarperCollins website address is www.**fire**and**water**.com

1 3 5 7 9 8 6 4 2

Text copyright © Kara May 1999
Illustrations copyright © Bob Harvey 1999

ISBN 000 694459 0

The author and illustrator assert the moral right to be
identified as the author and illustrator of the work.

Printed and bound in Great Britain by
Caledonian International Book Manufacturing Ltd, Glasgow G64

yeti boy

KARA MAY

Illustrations by Bob Harvey

Collins

An imprint of HarperCollins*Publishers*

PROLOGUE

The song of the bird came through the mist.
It was a tinkling sound like a silver bell. Fenn
put all his mind to listening to it.

The bird stopped singing.

Fenn stayed very still.

He was lying in tall grass. Beside him, a bush
blazed with red flowers.

Just beyond was an orange-check seat.

There was a suitcase, too, with things spilling out,
something yellow and something blue.

Further away, flames flickered.

Now Fenn remembered. The plane!

He must get to the plane. But he was bleeding a lot,
and couldn't move.

Fenn watched the flames leap higher.

The air was hot to breathe.

All he could hear was the roar.

He knew the explosion would come.

Fenn covered his head with his hands...
and waited.

1.

Fenn pushed open the flap of his tent. The mountains were still grey and wrapped in shadow. Tishaw, the head porter, was shouting and waving his arms about, trying to get the cook, Hensung, to clear up after breakfast. Breakfast?! Porridge with honey, no milk – unless you counted the powdered stuff – and tea, smoky from the fire.

Tishaw caught sight of him, and waved. Fenn pretended he hadn't noticed and drew back into his tent. He'd been awake since first light, eaten a hasty breakfast, and now he was waiting for the Kate woman and the others on the expedition to take themselves off for the day. There were eight of them, all scientists of some sort. The Kate woman had tried to get him to go with them.

'You can help set up the instruments, it's really interesting,' she said, all smiles. The others, too, had asked Fenn to join them. He saw them all 'making an effort' to jolly him along. He shrugged them off. He had his own plans for the day.

Fenn reached for his backpack, already packed with provisions from the store tent that he'd helped himself to – a bar of fruit and nut chocolate, an apple, a packet of raisins, and a hunk of what he called granite, which was supposed to be bread; it was tough to chew but it was filling. To wash it all down, he'd filled a water bottle with orange juice. He checked to make sure he'd fastened the top.

'That's everything,' he said.

He peered out of his tent once more. No sign of the Kate woman or the others. Time to go. He zipped up his anorak, so light it was like putting on a coat of feathers, but it kept out the cold and the bitterest wind. His anorak had a hood, and he wondered about the knitted woollen hat that made him feel he was wearing a tea cosy. Better take it. There was no wind now but it could suddenly whip down from the mountains where the snow hadn't yet melted. The camp was a few hours' walk from the snow line, Tishaw had told him, and today he was going to find it.

Tishaw and Hensung were sitting round the fire, arguing over a game they played with dice. They didn't notice Fenn as he tiptoed off, very deliberately in the opposite direction from the one taken by the scientists. He wished he had one of their laptops, though; he

could play computer games on it. 'She', the Kate woman, said she'd have one sent up for him with the next lot of supplies. He'd told her not to bother. He didn't want presents from her.

Fenn walked on quickly till he felt he was a good distance from the camp. So far he'd kept his eyes down, picking his way across the pebbles and grey gritty gravel that wound its way, like a path, between the scattering of rock and giant boulders. Now he looked up.

Around him, mountains soared up, their peaks white and glistening, like castles of icing sugar, topped with towers and turrets.

'The Sanaskars,' he breathed.

He'd heard about the Sanaskar Mountains for as long as he could remember. His dad, as a boy, had chanced on a book written in 1890 by the explorer, Rupert Evans, about his travels in the Sanaskars. From then on his dad was hooked. He'd got Mum enthused and Fenn had been fired up by them both. Most days one of them would come up with something they'd do, something they'd see: 'When we go to the Sanaskar Mountains.'

He didn't think Dad really believed they'd go, or Mum either. Fenn certainly didn't. For a start, it'd cost a fortune to get there. The Sanaskars were in the wild reaches of the Himalayas, in the heart of a small country called Asharn. The only way in was by foot or horse through treacherous mountain passes, or by light aircraft when weather conditions allowed it. Those who did manage to find a way there were turned back, more often than not, because they lacked the necessary entry permits. Not that most people were bothered! Asharn lacked all mod cons for the everyday tourist, and the Sanaskar Mountains were too challenging for the ordinary climber and not challenging enough for the experts who cluttered up Everest. But Fenn's father had told him he believed the Sanaskars was one of those rare, magical places in the world that had a special quality of its own.

'We'll soon find out. We're going!'

His dad dropped the news over tea.

Fenn thought he was joking.

'Ha! Ha! Pull the other one, Dad.'

Mum smiled. 'Fenn, it's true. Totally true!'

His dad's company had made an unexpected profit, and he'd got a huge bonus. That very same week a letter came from Kate Kildaire. She was Dad's cousin, quite a famous geologist, whose special interest was in ancient rocks; she believed they held the clue to the origins of the earth. Together with a small party of scientists, she'd managed to get a permit to go to Asharn to study for a few months. She thought she could obtain permits for Dad and Mum and Fenn if they wanted to go. Dad had cabled back an ecstatic YES!

'That Kate woman,' Fenn muttered. 'If she hadn't come interfering... No one had asked her.'

He kicked savagely at the ground, and a stone went flying. He ran quickly to retrieve it. It'd be just his luck if it was a saligram he was kicking away – a black stone with a fossil of a spiralling shellfish inside. But the stone was an ordinary grey one – not that anything here was ordinary. He was standing thousands of metres up, yet he was also on the seashore.

Fenn closed his eyes to imagine time rolling back hundreds, thousands, millions of years. As if on a screen in his mind, he saw two huge land masses edging towards each other across the sea between them. Closer, closer. Then the collision. The force of it pushed their rocky shores skywards. Wondering, he looked around once more. Those ancient rocky shores now flanked these very mountains, cut in with ravines and crevices that kept their mysteries to themselves, for the sun could not reach their depths. The Kate woman had tried to tell him about it. He'd soon cut her short.

'I know all that!' he told her.

The going was getting steep but there was an exciting prospect ahead – a glacier with its icy surface strewn with rocks that had fallen from craggy peaks, once washed by the sea. It was more than four hours since he'd left the camp – but it felt more like one hour, as if time had been eaten up in the vastness of the Sanaskars. He should hate them, he thought, but he didn't. They made him feel close to Mum and Dad. He could almost imagine they were with him.

'Hey, look!' he said, as if they could hear. 'I've done it! I've reached the snow line.'

Fenn scrambled on to find a place where he could put one foot in the snow and the other on bare rock.

The slopes that rose up around him were dusted with snow. And something else. Verglas! He grinned, chuffed that he knew the right word for the thin covering of ice that glossed over the treacherous holes and cracks in the rock. It was too dangerous to go any further. He looked round for somewhere to sit. This would do, he thought, choosing a small patch of grass that nestled between two pillars of granite, like the seat of a chair. The snow hadn't reached it, and it was sheltered and warmed by the sun.

He was famished. He munched his way through his supplies, pausing every now and then to take in the mountain spectacle around him. He was glad he was here on his own. There was no one he wanted to be with. Especially not her, the Kate woman, he thought grimly.

After the crash, she had radioed the hospital. He wouldn't speak to her, he wasn't speaking much to anyone. On the last occasion she'd phoned he happened to be in the room with Matron.

'When will you be coming to collect Fenn?' Matron asked. 'He is well enough now.'

Fenn was sitting by Matron, and he could hear the Kate woman's horrified squawk as it came through the receiver.

'I can't possibly look after him. I don't know anything about children.'

'He has no grandparents, Miss Kildaire. There is no one else.'

'But—'

Fenn didn't hear what came after the 'but', for Matron waved him out of the room.

He scowled at the icy expanse before him, just the way that he'd scowled when the Kate woman arrived at the hospital. She acted all lovey-dovey but he knew she didn't really want to look after him. He didn't care. He was glad. He had already decided to hate her. If it hadn't been for her, they wouldn't have come to the Sanaskars in the first place. The mountains would have stayed a wonderful dream which he shared with Mum and Dad. They'd be home together, right now, and he wouldn't have seen that plane on the edge of the airstrip, where a mangy goat, tied to a rope, was eating down the grass. The plane was to take them on the last stage of the journey from England. At his first sight of it, he knew it was going to crash.

'I won't think about it. There's no point,' he burst out.

He picked up his backpack and eased it on to his shoulders. The sun was beaming down, but once it went, the temperature would sink dramatically, and he'd become part of the frozen landscape if he didn't make a move. Already the wind was blowing up. He hoped he wouldn't have it against him as he made his way back. He looked round to gauge the direction it was coming from.

Then he saw the Yeti.

The Yeti was staring right at him.

'It has very brown eyes,' was Fenn's last thought before he was running, running, running.

He didn't see the sharp drop.

He was falling.

It was like the plane – falling, falling, all over again.

Fenn opened his eyes. The Yeti was bending over him, so close he could feel its breath. In terror Fenn backed away. Huge hairy arms reached out and gripped him. He struggled to break free. Then he saw where he was, on a narrow ledge, and an endless drop loomed below.

Fenn screamed aloud, screaming on and on.

The Yeti held him.

Held him fast.

Picked him up.

Slung him over its shoulder.

It was climbing, then it was running with remarkable speed.

Where was it taking him?

To its lair? To kill him, and eat him?!

'Do not fear, Human Boy.'

Fenn heard a whistling as soothing as a gentle sea.

Was he dreaming all this?

Was he dead?

If he was dead, would his body be hurting so much?

'Put the hurt in a bubble. Blow it away,' said the Yeti.

Softly, Fenn blew.

2.

The sun beamed into the cave. The earth floor was bare but the walls and ceiling were painted with patterns of bright colours. Above the entrance was a silver disc, oval in shape, with something engraved on it, but from where he lay Fenn couldn't see what it was.

He was lying on a bed of dried grass, with blankets of goatskins over him. How long had he been here? he wondered. His watch had been smashed in the fall and he had no way of telling. Through a haze of pain, he'd been aware of the Yeti looking after him – soothing the cuts with spiced smelling stuff that stung; bathing away the sweat of the fever; making him drink stuff that stank like mouldy leaves mixed with bad eggs.

Fenn stretched his legs. Then his arms. He was too weak to get up, but he was hungry. He looked round, and saw the Yeti, sitting on a bed like his own, in the shadow of the other side of the cave. He wasn't afraid of him now; the Yeti had shown him nothing but kindness. But he was wary, and edged away as the Yeti came and stood, peering at him.

'You want food,' he said. 'That is good. I will get what you need to start making you strong, Human Boy. What is it?' he asked at Fenn's startled look. 'Are your legs hurting again?'

'No, it's not that...' Fenn stammered. 'I thought I was imagining it before. But I can understand what you're saying!'

'And I understand your talking, Human Boy.'

'But how? You're speaking Yeti and I'm speaking my language, English!'

'It is so,' shrugged the Yeti, as if that was answer enough.

It must be a sort of telepathy we've got going, thought Fenn as the Yeti went off. Whatever it was, it would make things a lot easier that they could talk to each other.

Now he'd had the chance to have a closer look, the Yeti didn't exactly resemble the pictures he'd seen. His Yeti was very tall, and his forehead was broad, but not low. His feet were huge, with four wide toes, and the hair which covered his body was fine and silky. Fenn remembered his dad telling him that the local people's name for Yeti was 'The Long Hairs Who Keep To Themselves'. Not all the experts agreed they existed, but the locals swore to it. Well, now Fenn had seen one for himself.

He was living with a Yeti.

Talking to a Yeti!

'Or am I dreaming?' he said aloud.

He went so far as to pinch himself.

No, he wasn't dreaming!

Fenn pulled himself up and leant back against the wall, and for the first time he saw beyond the cave.

Grass – lush and green – stretched before him, spattered with red flowers on long orange stems. There were trees with fruit that looked like peaches. Peaches? In the wild, rocky Sanaskars? Impossible! Eager now to investigate further, Fenn tried to get up. His legs collapsed under him. He lay back, and adjusted his grass pillow.

He realised he wasn't alone.

Three Yeti were standing at the entrance of the cave, peering in at him. He couldn't quite grasp what they were saying. Their talk was punctuated by whistling sounds, which came to a sudden stop as a fierce whistling cut in over the top of them.

It was Fenn's Yeti. 'I have told you, the Human Boy is weak as a birdling. He is too sick for your chitter chatter.'

'I don't mind if they stay—,' began Fenn, not wanting to seem unfriendly. But his Yeti wasn't having it. He gave another fierce whistling and the others vanished.

'Eat, Human Boy.'

He offered a wooden plate that was set out with what looked like mashed potato, and a wooden cup. Fenn sniffed. No, not the compost-smelling stuff. He took a sip. Fruit juice, maybe peach or apricot. This was more like it!

'Eat. Drink. Everything!' said the Yeti.

There was no fork or spoon so Fenn used his fingers. Whatever he was eating tasted like potato, but with other things in it. The Yeti stood, looking down at him.

'Human Boy, I am Arkon,' he said. 'This Yeti is Arkon. I have this many big sunarounds.' He held up both hands, then eight fingers, and made a circling gesture with his hand.

'Arkon, hi!' grinned Fenn. He was catching on to this Yeti talk. A big sunaround was a year. Arkon was eighteen years old. 'I have twelve big sunarounds,' he said, holding up both hands, then two fingers. 'I am Fenn,' he added. 'My name is Fenn.'

'Fenn,' repeated Arkon, and gave a whistling.

'That's me, isn't it!' Fenn recognised himself at once. The whistling was describing him in a way that went beyond words.

'It's brilliant!' he enthused. 'Let me try and do a whistling of you.'

But how to describe Arkon?

He's kind and gentle in the way he looks after me, thought Fenn. But he's tough, and very strong, to have carried me over the mountains. I was unconscious most of the time, but we must have been on the move for days. Arkon was stubborn too, Fenn guessed, not one to be pushed around.

How do I put all that in a whistling? he wondered.

'You won't make good whistling like that, Human Boy!' Arkon copied his tensed-up face.

Fenn grinned. 'I'll learn this whistling thing, just you see.' He lay back, feeling suddenly sleepy. This was the longest he'd stayed awake since he'd come here. His eyes were closing but there was something he must say first.

Fenn remembered quite clearly now what had happened when he first saw Arkon. He remembered the fall. He remembered the feel of the rocky ledge which had broken his fall. He remembered the murky darkness of the drop below. If it hadn't been for Arkon… He shuddered.

'You saved my life, Arkon. Thank you.'

A troubled look crossed Arkon's face. But no, thought Fenn, I must have must have imagined it.

'You sleep, Human Boy. No more talking for now.'

'Are you always so bossy?' said Fenn, stifling a yawn.

Arkon looked suddenly serious. 'You are my Happening. It's for me to look after you. It is the Yeti way.'

'Me? A Happening? And what's the Yeti way?'

Arkon put his finger on his lips and closed his eyes. Fenn knew he'd get no answers from him then. He's stubborn, just as I thought, he said to himself as he drifted into sleep.

★

Fenn reached out, and picked up the plumpest of the apricots Arkon had left for him. He was feeling stronger with each day, or each small sunaround. He grinned to himself, pleased that he was catching on to Yeti expressions so quickly. Talking with Arkon was fun. And they didn't just talk. All morning they'd been telling whistling jokes. Fenn realised it wasn't his jokes, it was his whistling that made Arkon laugh!

It's brilliant we get on so well, thought Fenn, as he reached for another apricot. It's like we've been mates for ages. But there was something that puzzled and worried him. He could walk perfectly well now, but Arkon insisted that he stayed in bed. When asked, 'Why?' Arkon answered, 'Because it is best.' He wouldn't discuss it.

It doesn't make sense, Fenn frowned to himself. He was beginning to feel like a prisoner.

He flicked an apricot stone up in the air. He was going to catch it, but he left it to fall as the realisation struck. Of course! He should have thought of it before. Arkon wasn't keeping him in the cave as a *prisoner*. He was trying to protect him from something or someone *outside*. Fenn was sure he was right, and began to feel afraid. Lying there, in a sweat of fear, didn't help. He pushed back the goatskin. He was going to find out what this was about.

His legs were wobbly, but it wasn't surprising after goodness knows how long in bed. Fenn reached out for the cave wall to steady himself, and eased his way along it.

Arkon blocked his way.

'Quickly,' he whispered, and pointed to the bed.

Fenn hesitated, but only for a second. The look on Arkon's face, together with a whistling that conjured up a coming storm, left him in no doubt that there was some kind of danger. His heart was pounding against his chest as he scrambled under the coverlet. Arkon sat on the floor beside him. His face was too calm to be natural, and Fenn felt even more frightened.

A shadow appeared at the cave entrance. Fenn steeled himself, expecting something fearsome. To his astonishment, it was a Yeti girl who walked in. She was strikingly good-looking and about seventeen, he guessed.

What's going on? Fenn wondered as Arkon went to greet her.

3.

'Ruala, this is the Human Boy,' said Arkon, with a friendly smile.

'Hullo, Ruala,' Fenn ventured.

But Ruala ignored him, and turned to Arkon.

'I have a message from the Most Ancient,' she said. 'The meeting begins when the sun is over the Meeting Place Tree. You are to bring *that* with you.' She nodded in Fenn's direction, but did not look at him.

'The Human Boy is still too weak,' protested Arkon. 'He needs more time to recover his strength. I'll come alone.'

Ruala gave a whistling, sharp as a whip. Her eyes

narrowed. Her look was cold. 'The meeting is about to begin. You will be there, and the Human too. It is time, the Most Ancient said.'

'Ruala—' Arkon began. But she had already turned on her heel and left. Fenn could still feel the chill she brought with her.

'What is this meeting, Arkon? It's something to do with me, isn't it?'

'Not only you – me too, Human Boy. They are upset because I brought you here. They let you stay when it seemed you would die. But now you are almost better, the meeting is to sort things out, that is all,' Arkon shrugged, making light of it. But Fenn wasn't convinced. If the other Yeti were like Ruala, he didn't like to imagine what 'sorting things out' might mean.

'Don't get in a worry. You leave it all to this Yeti.' Arkon thumped his chest. 'Come, we go now.'

Fenn blinked in the sunlight after so long indoors. The valley stretched into the distance, and snow-capped mountains rose up all around.

Just ahead, three Yeti stood staring. Now what? wondered Fenn, edging closer to Arkon.

The tallest Yeti was also the broadest, with muscles like a weight lifter. His companion was quite skinny. The hair on his head was streaked orange, and stuck up, like spikes, which gave him a comic look. Beside him was a young child, a girl, whose hair was braided with flowers.

Arkon beckoned them over.

'You can see, this Human Boy is no more than a scrap!' he said, and followed it with a jokey whistling.

Fenn realised he was trying to win them over. 'Hi,' he said, doing his best to look both cool and friendly.

The big Yeti continued to stare as if he'd swallowed something and he couldn't puzzle out what it was. But the other, with the orange streaks, came up and walked around Fenn, scrutinising him from head to toe.

'If you go much closer, Human Boy will start scratching.' Arkon gave a whistling that conjured up a jumping flea. 'Human Boy, this is Cheb. And that mighty big Yeti is Burso.' He turned to the child. But she didn't wait to be introduced.

'I am Isa.' She followed her name with a whistling that sounded to Fenn like bubbles, floating about in the air. For some moments, she gazed at him, looking directly into his eyes.

Suddenly she took a sprig of flowers from her hair.

'For you, Human Boy.'

On impulse, Fenn stuck the flowers behind his ear. Isa jumped about, whistling in delight. Cheb and Burso followed when she ran off to join the Yeti who had already gathered nearby. They were sitting in a circle and they were all looking at Fenn. His anxiety moved up a gear when he heard a whiplash whistling behind him.

Ruala!

Maybe she wasn't as horrible as she'd seemed on first meeting. He attempted a smile as she passed. She gave him the big-freeze look. Arkon went towards her, holding out his hand. Ruala froze him off, too. Fenn couldn't hear what she was saying, but he could guess from the tone of her voice as she spoke to the Yeti in the circle. The glances that turned towards Arkon and himself became increasingly suspicious and hostile.

Suddenly a silence fell. Fenn's gaze followed that of the others. He saw a bent figure approach. He didn't need Arkon to tell him that it was the Most Ancient. She looked as if she'd been alive since the world began. Her hair was grey as stone and her face was carved deep with wrinkles. Isa ran forward, and assisted her to a polished log seat.

'The meeting is now,' said Arkon softly. 'Come.' He put his arm round Fenn's shoulder, and led him towards the circle.

No place was set out for them. Cheb and Burso moved apart, and Arkon and Fenn sat between them.

What's everyone waiting for? thought Fenn. Glancing around the circle, he guessed there must be about a hundred Yeti, and they all sat, not moving. Their stillness was unnerving.

Then at last the Most Ancient gave a whistling. Fenn noticed that the sun was poised over a tree behind her that looked as ancient as she.

'You are all here. I thank you.' The Most Ancient spoke without raising her voice but she commanded the circle; every eye was fixed upon her.

'Arkon,' she said.

Arkon rose to his feet as she addressed him.

'You know the for why of this meeting?'

He nodded.

'You have gone against our Yeti way, have you not?'

He lowered his gaze.

'I ask you, Arkon, what is our way towards Humans?'

His head was still lowered. 'To have no contact with them, not by seeing or hearing even.'

'That is so. And for why?'

'Because—' he broke off. 'But everyone knows,' he burst out.

'But you let it fall into forgetting,' said the Most Ancient. 'You forgot our way. I shall remind you of what you forgot:

'The Ones Who Came First, long before, told us that we are *like* Humans, but not the same. They gave warning that our way is not theirs, and that the Yeti must keep to themselves.

'Fenn, Human Boy.'

Fenn realised the Most Ancient was speaking directly to him. He jumped to his feet and began to move towards her. It was as if she had summoned him.

'Please, stay sitting,' said the Most Ancient.

Thankfully, Fenn sat down again. The Most Ancient was immensely old but he could feel the power of her presence. He felt, too, she was able to see deep inside him. He wasn't sure how to face her. Copying Arkon, Fenn looked down as she spoke to him.

'Do you know our Yeti way, Fenn?' asked the Most Ancient.

He couldn't begin to imagine. He shook his head.

'I wish you to understand, so I shall tell you,' said the Most Ancient. She paused, then went on: 'Our Yeti way is to be as we are, and not to have longing to be who or what we are not. We share what we have, and take from each other only what is given.'

The Most Ancient gestured to the valley around them. 'All this is our place. The water is sweet, the sun shines from our waking to our sleeping. All that we need is here and we have no longing for what we have not.'

'Yes, that is our way,' said the rest of the Yeti, and set up a whistling.

'Is it your Human way also, Fenn?' asked the Most Ancient as the whistling faded away.

'I don't think it is,' he whispered.

'I can tell you it isn't!' blazed Ruala.

She sprang to her feet and turned in a fury on Arkon. 'You have lost the power of your thinking to bring that Human here! He will bring others. Then what? They will take us from here, or kill us!'

Shouts and alarmed whistlings spread around the circle like the wind gathering speed. The Most Ancient held up her hand and her whistling silenced the others.

'Let Arkon speak,' she said. 'Arkon, what do you say?'

What *could* Arkon say? thought Fenn. He'd already admitted he'd broken the Yeti way by bringing him here. The Yeti were against them both, Ruala had made sure of that. But if Arkon was afraid, he gave no sign of it. Which was just as well, shivered Fenn. He was scared enough for them both.

4.

The breeze brushed the branches of the tree behind the Most Ancient. Arkon could feel her gaze, waiting for him to speak, but he knew she would not hurry him. He did not know what he was going to say; when he was ready, the words would come.

He looked around the circle. His eye paused at Ruala. She glared back at him. He did not blame her for it; he understood her feeling all too well. He had not meant to bring the Human here.

Before Fenn, Arkon hadn't seen a Human. None of the Yeti had seen one, he thought, except perhaps the Most Ancient, and Ruala of course. There was something about Ruala that was like the boy. One

moment, she was blazing like a fire fed with dry sticks.
Then, she would be very quiet, as if she was scratched
raw inside, hurting too much to speak of it. Fenn, too,
was one thing, and then another. When he was up and
about, he seemed quite happy. But at night, he screamed
out in his sleep, whimpered and wept. At first Arkon
believed it was from the injuries from the fall. They were
almost healed, but Fenn still cried in his sleep, and like
Ruala, his eyes held a heavy sorrow.

What would the meeting decide about the boy?
Arkon wondered. Whatever it was, he would follow it.
That is the Yeti way, he thought. He had broken it, by
bringing the boy here. He hadn't meant to. It had just
happened.

I shall tell them the how of it, Arkon decided. It is
the best hope to keep the boy safe.

'I was on a wander-about,' said Arkon, addressing
the circle at last. 'I was following my feet where they
took me. They took me to a place where I had been
before. Some of you have been there also. I was
looking for where the snow leaves the rocks to
themselves. Suddenly I see the boy. I am about to go
quickly. But the wind, which has been silent, suddenly
howls. The boy looks up. He has sighting of me. His
fear is like that of a mouse who sees before it the
mighty snow leopard!'

Arkon gave a whistling. The Yeti gasped at the fear it
invoked.

'Go on, Arkon,' said the Most Ancient.

'The boy runs fast. Just beyond, the ground gives

way to the air. But he cannot see through his fearing of me. He runs on, and he falls—'

'He falls,' echoed the Yeti.

'The crevice is so deep I think it has swallowed him. But a ledge, not wide, catches him.'

'How you could tell?' Ruala leapt up, accusing. 'You went to look, didn't you?'

'I went to see if he had any life in him.'

'That is against our way,' she flashed back. 'You should have taken yourself out of his sight.'

'It was because of me that he fell, Ruala. I went only to take him from the ledge, away from the danger of another falling.'

'So, you bring him here, to our place!'

'If I had not made him fall, I would have left him. I did not mean to have sighting of him, or he of me. It just happened! It was a Happening,' insisted Arkon. 'Look, you can see. He is just a boy. He cannot harm us.'

'But what of those who come seeking him?' scathed Ruala. 'They will follow your tracks.'

The Yeti turned on Arkon with angry whistlings.

'I covered my tracks!' he protested. 'Also, I made rock-falls behind me. The Humans cannot follow.'

But the angry whistlings grew louder until the Most Ancient held up her hand. At once there was silence.

'Now the boy is here, Arkon,' she said, 'what is to be done with him? Have you considered that?'

The question deflated him. His shoulders drooped, and he shook his head.

'The boy is as weak as a birdling now,' said Burso, speaking slowly to let his thoughts form. 'But what will happen when he gets his strength? He will find his way back to the Humans. Like Ruala says, he will bring them here.'

'Yes! And then what? We know already!' Ruala turned for support from the circle. Again, they started the angry whistling.

Fenn gripped his hands round his knees to try and hold himself together. He knew where this was heading. They were going to kill him!

'I wouldn't tell anyone if you asked me not to. I wouldn't bring anyone here,' he trembled.

'You would say that, Human Boy! What else would you say!'

The Most Ancient gestured Ruala to be silent, but she took no notice and blazed on.

'Remember the warning of the Ones Who Came First! They tell us we are safe as long as we keep to ourselves. We know what Humans do to Yeti!'

Ruala gave a whistling.

It conjured up a terrifying menace.

The Yeti covered their faces, and moaned, rocking themselves back and forth.

'Let Arkon take the boy to where he found him,' declared Cheb. 'He has no strength to find his way back to us or to go and tell the others. He must live on the mountain and take his chance.'

'Yes, take him back! Now, at once!'

'Arkon?' said the Most Ancient. 'What do you say?'

'The boy will not make the journey, Most Ancient. You may as well kill him now. But that's not the Yeti way! Also,' Arkon pressed on, 'the Humans will be looking for him, as we'd search for one of our own who was missing. If I take him back at once, they may have a sighting not just of him, but of me.'

'That is so,' said the Most Ancient.

The Yeti murmured amongst themselves.

'We cannot kill the boy!'

'We cannot take him back!'

'But he is a danger if he stays!'

They looked towards the Most Ancient, seeking her guidance.

'My thinking is this,' she said. 'We let time pass so the Humans will lose hope for the boy, and no longer search. Then Arkon will take him to where he found him. Until then, the boy stays, if you agree.'

The Most Ancient surveyed the circle.

Under her gaze, no one felt like objecting – until she came to Ruala.

'I say the Human must go at once!'

But she was the only one.

'It is therefore decided, the boy shall stay with us, for the now,' said the Most Ancient. She pointed to a tree, just beyond, with strips of white bark hanging from it. 'When the sun exactly reaches the White Bark Tree, Arkon shall return the boy to the place he found him.'

'It shall be so,' Arkon assured her.

'You have the care of the boy, Arkon. He is your Happening, and that is our way. It is also our way,' the Most Ancient added, drawing everyone's attention to her, 'to make good of what is decided. I ask you not to let that slip into forgetting.

'Human Boy!'

The Most Ancient beckoned. Fenn went and stood before her. He'd been convinced the Yeti were going to kill him. Now he expected at least a warning or a rebuke. But the Most Ancient's words wafted gently over him.

'You are safe here. Let your fear go. Let the breeze take it. You are safe with the Yeti.'

Now it was Arkon's turn to be summoned.

'You have caused upset, Arkon. You know that. Is there anything you are wanting to say?' asked the Most Ancient.

'I am wanting to say,' said Arkon, 'I am sorry for the upset. To all Yeti here, this very next small sunaround, I shall bring water from the river and the sweetest roots from the earth. I am hoping it will help take the upset away.'

A burst of cheers, claps and whistlings rose up from the circle. But not from Ruala. She turned a fierce look on Arkon, and stalked off.

'Let her be,' said the Most Ancient, making a smoothing movement with both hands. Then she stood up and gave a single whistling.

'The meeting is over, Human Boy,' said Arkon, beaming.

'You mean, that's it?' Fenn couldn't believe it. For a second time, Arkon had saved his life – he'd never have survived, back on that mountain. But now he was safe! The Most Ancient had said so herself.

Fenn went to thank Arkon, but he just laughed. 'Look, here is Isa, wanting to talk to you.'

'It is good that you stay, Human Boy,' Isa smiled up at him.

'But you want more fat on you, or the wind will carry you away,' grinned Burso, as he strolled up.

'Like this!' said Cheb, and gave a whistling like a blustering wind.

Arkon put his arm round Fenn's shoulder.

'Soon I will have this Human Boy as big and strong as me! Well, not quite so big and strong!'

They all laughed.

Now it was agreed Fenn could stay, the Yeti crowded around with friendly smiles and whistlings, eager for Arkon to introduce them. Fenn was relieved their hostility had melted so quickly. But he must help Arkon get the roots and the water for the upset.

'Can I?' he asked. 'Is it allowed?'

'You make the offer,' grinned Arkon, 'so I can take it! Are you good with a digging stick, Human Boy?'

'Digging stick? What is it exactly?'

Arkon thought Fenn was joking, then realised he wasn't.

'I learn you. I learn you to be like a Yeti, if you want.'

'Yes, I'll try,' said Fenn. He realised, for the first time since the plane crash, that he didn't feel totally, desperately miserable. He hoped the sun would take a long time to reach the White Bark Tree.

5.

Fenn woke the next morning to find Arkon was missing. He appeared soon after. It was still early, but he'd been up since first light to begin the promised deliveries of water.

'You said I could help,' Fenn protested.

'There is plenty more for you to do, Human Boy.'

They traipsed to the river, back and forth, carrying the water in sunbaked clay pots. They were received in silence, not even a whistling, just an acknowledging nod or a smile. Not by Ruala, however. She grabbed the waterpot from Arkon and hurled the contents over him.

'I want nothing from you or that Human!'

'Good! One less person to get roots for,' Fenn muttered. But Ruala was out to make trouble. He would have to be on his guard.

At last the water was delivered. Fenn was aching all over, but he'd given his word that he'd help with the water and the roots and he was going to stick to it. He'd been surprised and very relieved that no one, not even Ruala, had demanded that Arkon should be punished for breaking the Yeti way. It had been left to Arkon himself to decide what he should do to make up for the upset he'd caused.

'What if you didn't offer to do anything? Or if you did, then forgot? Or couldn't be bothered?' Fenn asked.

Arkon shook his head, seeming perplexed by the question. 'I must do it, so I do it. Now, this is for you.' He handed Fenn a stout stick and informed him that it was a digging stick.

If this was what he had to dig with, the Yeti would be waiting for their roots forever, thought Fenn. The wretched stick kept slipping. But at last he began to get the knack of it.

'This root looks like a whopper, Arkon.'

In his excitement, Fenn dug more quickly.

'Is whopper going to run away, Human Boy?'

Fenn grinned. 'I don't think so. It hasn't got any legs!'

'Then what's the hurry? Slow down, or you'll bruise it. These are for the Most Ancient.'

Carefully, Fenn added the root – and it *was* a whopper – to the others in the grass-woven basket. 'You take these, Arkon.'

'I took the water. Have your legs got no strength for walking?'

'It's not that. It's just…'

'You are scared of the Most Ancient!'

'Not really… But don't you feel the same?'

Arkon smiled. 'But that is between you and me. Now, are you coming? Or do you stay hiding away, like a birdling with no feathers?'

The Most Ancient's cave was behind a screen of trees. She was standing in the entrance and seemed to know they were coming.

Arkon offered the basket.

'You bring us so many good things,' she said. 'The upset is over, all taken away.'

'That is my hoping,' said Arkon. 'Fenn helped me,' he added. 'That root is of his digging.'

The Most Ancient smiled. 'Already you learn our Yeti ways, Fenn. You are our Yeti Boy now.' She reached out and touched his shoulder. He felt himself glow at her touch as if she had lit a spark that filled him all through with light. He walked away, his head reeling.

'Arkon, you heard what she called me!'

'I heard!'

He shouted it out so everyone could hear.

'This boy is Yeti Boy now. The Most Ancient says so herself!'

Isa danced around Fenn. 'You like to be Yeti Boy, yes?'

'It's brilliant!' He gave an enthusiastic whistling. Then… 'Oh, oh,' Fenn muttered. He'd felt Ruala's hating gaze before he saw her. He spun round, and there she was, in the shadow of the trees. What was it with her? he wondered. But he wasn't going to let her spoil things.

Pointedly, he turned his back on her.

Fenn was on his way to join Arkon, Burso and Cheb at the water hole. They were becoming an inseparable foursome. Isa called them The Big Noise because of the racket they made, fooling about. It's great that we're mates already, thought Fenn.

He spotted a sharp stone on the track and jumped over it. Then he went back and deliberately trod on it. He was barefooted, but he didn't feel even a prick. For some days he'd been rubbing on a concoction of leaves and tree sap that Isa had made for him. It ponged like manure, but it had made the soles of his feet tough as she had promised. Even though she was young, she knew what plants to use for what. All the Yeti were the same, he'd discovered. They seemed to have been born with the knowledge in them, like human child prodigies who could do difficult maths and write music. He was no prodigy, thought Fenn, as he reached the water hole, but he *was* becoming an expert swimmer!

Arkon and Cheb were high up on the bank. On their knees, they were blowing the glowing embers of a fire into action. Burso was not far away, prodding at the ground with his digging stick. Fenn left them to it. He wanted to have a go at his latest craze – his Tarzan act. He climbed the tree at the water's edge, gripped the vine that dangled from it, and swung himself out. Then he let go to make a splash. The water stung his backside as he bombed into it.

Fenn dived on down, and began to gather up stones from the river bed. Maybe this time he'd find a saligram. When his breath gave out, he clambered up on the bank and inspected his hoard, hoping to find a black stone amongst them. But no luck! The stones were all grey.

'You can't eat those! Come, Yeti Boy! We have food!' called Burso.

Fenn's eyes widened in horror as Burso picked out one of the creepy-crawlies that wriggled and writhed in a heap. He stunned it with a stone, and threaded it on to a stick to roast.

'I do not believe it, Burso! You're not eating that!'

'It's a good eater. I cook it for you, Yeti Boy.'

Creepy-crawly kebab? No thanks. But Fenn was hungry.

'I'd sooner have fish.'

'So have fish!' Arkon pointed to the river that flowed on beyond the water-hole.

'He's going to catch a fish,' grinned Cheb.

Burso sat back and folded his arms. 'Catch fish for us too, Yeti Boy.'

They sat back to watch as if they were at a circus. He was the clown, thought Fenn, wishing he'd kept his mouth shut.

Fish were the only living creatures the Yeti killed

for food – except for creepy-crawlies. Fenn hadn't seen any animals about, apart from wild cats and the goats that sometimes strayed down from the mountains. If the Yeti found a dead one, they skinned it, but they would never kill one themselves. They took eggs, one only, from each nest of wingless brown birds – smaller than hens but larger than chickens – which they found where the grass grew tall. Fenn was becoming skilled in finding them himself. But fishing! The Yeti made it look so easy. They walked into the water. Next thing, they were grasping a fish.

Maybe he'd do it this time.

He stood so he wouldn't cast a shadow – at least he'd remembered that! He saw a flash of silver. He lunged, and fell on his face with a splash.

The others were laughing so much they held their hands round their ribs to stop them aching. 'What do your Elders say that you've got so big and can't catch a fish, Yeti Boy?'

'Okay, so I'm a comedy turn,' said Fenn. 'But we get our fish from a supermarket.' How to explain supermarket? 'It's like a big cave, full of food, not just fish,' he said. 'We go and take what we want, and pay for it with—' He broke off to think of an explanation for money. But no one was interested. 'It's the Human way,' pronounced Cheb, and they were content to leave it at that.

Fenn puzzled, not for the first time, that the Yeti were bafflingly uncurious. Not just about him and the world he came from. He'd tried to find out more about the Ones Who Came First, mentioned by the Most Ancient. The reply he received was, 'They were here before the Yeti', but who they were, or where they'd gone to, nobody knew or seemed motivated to find out. Their curiosity gene must be missing, he thought. It wasn't missing in him. He couldn't resist having a taste of creepy-crawly kebab to see what it was like.

He took a tiny bite, ready to spit it out. But – hey! It was tasty, like a cross between prawns and chicken. 'Okay, you were right, it's not bad. I don't mind having another.'

Arkon handed him the digging stick.

'Changed my mind,' said Fenn quickly. Eating a creepy-crawly kebab was one thing. Digging up the squiggly white grubs was something else.

'Anyone for apricots?' he asked. 'Okay, I'll get some.' The best tree Fenn knew was near the cave and the others said they'd meet him there.

Fenn gathered as many apricots as he could carry. It was hotting up, and he was glad to be out of the sun for a while. It was cool in the cave, and the water, which they kept in a clay pot, was refreshingly sweet. He gulped some down, replaced the woven grass cover, and was on his way outside when his eyes fell on the silver disc above the entrance.

He reached up and took the disc from the wall. He'd been meaning to have a closer look at it since he'd first arrived.

'Wow! This is something else!' breathed Fenn.

Engraved on the disc, unmistakably, was Arkon. He was holding a flaming torch to a pyramid of spears. Fenn had never seen any of the Yeti with a spear, but it wasn't *what* was engraved that held him, awed and wondering — it was the quality of the workmanship.

'It's good, yes?' said Arkon, as he came in.

Fenn smoothed his fingers over the engraving. He felt a tingling as if it had life in it. 'However did you make it?'

'This Yeti didn't make it,' laughed Arkon. 'The sun and moon fall out of the sky before I know how to begin! It is the Keepers who made it. They make this also.' He fetched another engraving from by his bed that Fenn hadn't noticed. It showed Arkon, lying on his back, by the water hole where they'd been not long before; he was gazing up at the sky, with a blissed-out expression.

'I was so happy, Yeti Boy.'

'Yes I can see. But why?'

'I don't know for why. It just happened. It was a Happening.'

'What exactly is a Happening?' asked Fenn. 'You said I was one at the meeting.'

'A Happening is what happens, of course. Some Happenings you want to remember. You go to the Keepers and tell them about it and they make these.' Arkon gestured to the engravings. 'The Keepers have made many for me. I take them back when I can remember the Happenings without them, or a new Happening comes that I want to remember more. The Keepers have all our Happenings from the beginning.'

44

'From the beginning of the Yeti? I'd love to see them.' Fenn was curious not just to see the engraved Happenings but to meet the Keepers who made them with such extraordinary skill.

'Where do the Keepers live, Arkon? Will you take me there?'

'I take you if the time comes,' he said vaguely, with that absent look he developed when Fenn asked a question he couldn't or didn't want to answer. 'But the time of the Spear Contest comes very soon. The big sunaround just before, I win, so I light the Spear Fire.'

Arkon pointed to himself on the engraving, by the pyramid of spears. 'It is my best Happening. I like it so much, I am thinking to win again!'

'Yes, like you keep saying!' said Cheb, who'd come with Burso to join them. 'Come on, let's go outside.'

They sat in the shade, and munched through the apricots. Then Arkon handed round pieces of a root which he claimed made the Yetis' hair so that it kept them cool in the sun and warm in the cold. Fenn stared at his legs as if he expected them to sprout long hairs any minute. It was too hot for trousers – he was wearing undershorts and his T-shirt. Both were ragged and torn where he'd snagged them. But so what? He didn't have to bother about that sort of thing.

He looked out across the valley, bright with flowers and fruit trees. The mountains towered in the distance. On the other side was another world. Not his world, not any more. There was no going back to his old life. It was shattered and gone forever.

Suddenly, Fenn knew he wanted stay here with the Yeti. The only problem he could see was Ruala. But she'd been overruled before. Everyone else liked him. Somehow, he'd persuade them to let him stay after the sun reached the White Bark Tree.

'I'll never look at that tree again!' vowed Fenn.

He'd forget the Kate woman, blank her out forever, and everything else that had gone before – this was his place now.

He had the Spear Contest to look forward to.

He would meet the mysterious Keepers.

He would do all Yeti things.

Fenn jumped to his feet.

'I am Yeti Boy!' he called out, and followed it with a jubilant whistling that floated off and about the valley.

6.

It was late afternoon when Kate Kildaire realised that she hadn't seen Fenn since breakfast. She wasn't too worried. He'd taken himself off for hours at a time before. It wasn't good for him to be on his own so much, but he wouldn't let anyone near him for more than a few minutes. Her attempts to talk to him, to try and bring him out of himself, always got the same response – he turned his back and walked away, giving off vibes that unmistakably said: Keep Off. In a way, Kate was relieved. She didn't know what to say to him – what could she possibly say to a boy who'd suddenly lost both his parents?

Fenn had made it obvious from the outset that he didn't like her. She didn't blame him. As a stand-in mother and father she was a total loss. She knew nothing about children. Even as a child herself, she'd been a loner, absorbed every spare moment by her fascination with rocks. The thought that rocks held the history of the world from its earliest beginnings thrilled her. Cousin James was rather like her, though more light-hearted, in his obsession with the Sanaskar Mountains. She remembered he'd promised himself that one day he'd go there. When the expedition was set up she was glad to use her contacts to help him. The permits had cost her a small fortune, though she hadn't told him that, and she could afford it more easily than he. After all these years, she was looking forward to seeing him and Alice; Fenn too. They were the only family she had now.

Kate's work was based in the States and somehow the years had slipped by. She hadn't seen James or Alice since their wedding and it would be her first meeting with Fenn. In the latest photograph they had sent her, Fenn stood by his new mountain bike, with a grin that held the promise of mischief. He looked very much like James at that age.

At the hospital, when Matron had brought Fenn to meet her, she thought there'd been a mistake. This ashen-faced boy with a tight set mouth and eyes that stared coldly at her – Fenn?

As if he'd read her thoughts, 'I am Fenn,' he said.

Looked her up and down.

And walked out of the room.

They found him standing on the hospital steps, holding his backpack. 'Where are we going?' he had asked, mocking her, challenging, as if he guessed she had no idea.

And he was right, thought Kate.

At the time, she was still in a state of shock herself. She hadn't thought further than collecting Fenn from the hospital. But perhaps, without knowing, she'd already decided. It had taken years to get the funding for the expedition to the Sanaskars. The opportunity wouldn't come again. It was truly a chance of a lifetime.

'I'm taking you with me, to the base camp where I'm working. You can be part of our team,' Kate had told him, trying to enthuse Fenn with a smile. 'You'll need mountaineering clothes and boots. I'll have them sent from Delhi. As soon as they arrive, we'll go.' It was a day's drive to the nearest village, where she would hire porters and a guide. 'Then it's a three-day trek,' she went brightly on.

Kate paused to give Fenn an opportunity to say something.

Fenn just stood, staring past her.

'Shall I carry that for you?' Kate had asked, uncomfortable in his silence. She reached out to take his backpack. He had tightened his grip on it and stared through her.

'I should have tried harder with him,' Kate said, now desperate to find Fenn. 'It's my fault he's gone. If he's lost—'

The other scientists tried to reassure her. 'He'll be back. He knows it's dangerous to go far from the camp. We'll set up a search if it makes you feel easier.'

They asked Tishaw to organise it.

Now the men who carried their luggage and cooked for them were in charge, and the scientists, in their anxiety for the missing boy, did precisely as they were ordered. They were fearful for Kate, as well as for Fenn. Not even the death of her cousin James and his wife had taken away her cool air of detachment. But in the hours since Fenn had been found missing, it was as if she'd been blasted apart inside. Kate couldn't stop crying.

A shout from Tishaw startled her back to herself.

'Look, Missy!'

He led her to an overhang of rock which the new fall of snow had yet to reach. He pointed to a blood-stained indent.

'Boy,' he said.

Then, he pointed again.

'Footprints. Long hair. Yeti!'

Amongst the porters, there was a babble of excitement.

'Leave off,' hissed a tall man with round pebbled glasses, the meteorologist on the expedition. 'You're only making it worse for Kate. Yeti don't exist.' He glanced at the footprint. A particularly large specimen of mountain ape or, he shuddered, a mountain bear or lion.

It was getting dark. There was nothing further they could do till morning, and they returned to the camp.

Kate called Tishaw aside. 'Tell me about the Yeti. Have you ever seen one?'

Tishaw nodded.

'What happened?'

'I see him. He run. I follow. But then—'

'Go on.'

'He is suddenly gone.'

'Gone? What do you mean?'

'He is gone. Into the rock.'

'Into a tunnel, a cave?'

Tishaw shook his head. 'Into the rock. The rock is solid like a wall.'

'And the Yeti walked through it?'

'Yes,' said Tishaw, not troubled by her sarcastic tone, 'others will tell you the same.' He paused. 'You don't believe me, Missy, because I'm not a person with much education like you.' There was no bitterness, just resignation in his voice. 'You heard about Mr Jack Hubbert?'

Kate had heard a colleague mention the name. 'He's a mountaineer, isn't he?'

'Not climb now. Avalanche. Broke leg. Leg never get better. He comes back, just to be here. Because he loves the Sanaskars. Jack Hubbert will tell you about Yeti. Jack Hubbert has seen Yeti too.'

'Could you send someone to fetch him? Tell Hubbert I'll pay him.'

Tishaw shook his head at her, as if she'd missed the point. 'Hubbert will come, Missy. When I tell him about the boy and the Yeti, he will come.'

A few days later, a cheerful bellow burst over the camp: Jack Hubbert had arrived. He was tall and thick set, his face tanned by sun and snow, with eyes blue as a mountain lake in summer. At once, Hubbert put himself in charge. None of the others objected, but it annoyed Kate, even though he had come on her behalf. He was a rough and ready type, she thought, and arrogant with it. She wanted to put him straight from the start.

'I'm a scientist, Hubbert. I don't believe this Yeti nonsense.'

Kate broke off. Hubbert was grinning as if he was trying to hold back his laughter, and she was the joke. 'Whether you believe they exist or not, it won't bother the Yeti. My research suggests that they prefer it that way. Is the footprint still there?'

'We put a polythene frame over it to keep the snow off. Whatever it is, it's an unusual specimen.'

'Specimen? And what sort of specimen are you, Katie Kildaire?'

'Kate, it's Kate,' she said firmly. She regretted sending for Hubbert. She'd done so when she'd been too distressed to think straight. Now he was talking to Tishaw in his own dialect.

'When you're ready,' she said.

'Yes, we need to get moving. Let's go – Kate,' added Hubbert, with a small bow. She eyed him coldly, and told Tishaw to lead the way.

First, Hubbert examined the spot where they assumed Fenn had fallen.

'If the ledge hadn't broken his fall… But luck was with him. It's a good sign. In the Sanaskars, luck is either on your side, or against you. By rights, that avalanche should have finished *me* off, but here I am!'

'To state the obvious,' put in Kate.

'To state the obvious again,' Hubbert grinned at her, 'the footprint was made by a Yeti.'

'There! I tell you, Missy!' crowed Tishaw.

'However, I'll be frank with you, Kate, I've never heard tell of a Yeti taking off with a human. Here, take it easy.' Kate had gone horribly white. 'If, just for the sake of argument, it *was* a Yeti, and it took Fenn away,' her voice trembled. 'What would it... ' She couldn't bring herself to ask the question but Hubbert knew what was in her mind.

'I'm a straightforward man, and I'd tell you if I thought otherwise. But in all my years in the Sanaskars, I've not come across a single story of a Yeti doing harm to anyone, human or otherwise. Yeti aren't animals, Kate. The one I saw — it was only for an instant — was a gentle-looking soul. It talked to me, as it happens.'

'Talked to you!'

'Talked to me,' repeated Hubbert.

'Oh yes? And what did it say?' Kate couldn't believe he was serious.

'It looked at me, right in the eye, and said, "It is not the time."'

'Time for what?'

'Now you're asking. I don't know. But that's what it said.'

'I don't believe a word of this, Hubbert.'

He laughed. 'I wouldn't expect you to. But I'll tell you something, Katie Kildaire; my hunch is that Fenn is alive. The boy obviously fell. Could be the Yeti took him somewhere to shelter for the night. I know the best guides and trackers hereabouts. I'll get a search party together. If that's okay by you?'

'Thanks.' The word came with a struggle. She didn't believe in the Yeti, she couldn't see how Fenn could survive in the low night temperatures of the Sanaskars, and Jack Hubbert was the last person she'd choose to ask for help. But he offered her hope that Fenn was alive.

Each day brought new arrivals to the camp, all eager to join the search and earn the money that was being offered as a reward. There was even promise of a bonus for whoever found Fenn. Kate viewed them with dismay. Most of them looked like bandits and cut-throats.

'You can't trust them, Hubbert. Even I can see that.'

'I'm not saying they wouldn't slit my throat for the clothes on my back. But I trust them to bring Fenn safely back. The reward will guarantee that. And they know the mountains.'

Hubbert knew that others would come to the camp, more interested in the Yeti footprint than searching for Fenn. But Kate had enough to concern her, he thought, so he didn't mention it.

7.

Fenn was excited by the prospect of the Spear Throwing Contest – until he realised he was expected to take part in it.

'It is for everyone,' Arkon informed him, 'excepting for babies and Elders.'

'But I've never thrown a spear in my life!'

'So now you can start, Yeti Boy.'

There was worse to come. Like everyone else, Fenn had to make his own spear. At last, he'd managed it. But the contest was about who could throw the furthest, and so far, his spear just flopped at his feet. He saw Arkon struggling not to laugh.

'All right, Arkon. Ha ha! But I'm new to this, remember!'

'I learn you again, Yeti Boy. Keep your eye on the faraway, yes? Where your eye goes, the spear will follow.'

'If only it would!' muttered Fenn, as Arkon left him to practice. 'I'll try some whistling, maybe that'll help.'

He was really into the whistling. The Yeti used it in all sorts of ways. It could be to urge them on to do something, to express something where words weren't enough, or just for the fun of it, like in the evenings, when they sat round the fires. It was riveting how, without a word being said, they could build up – not pictures, exactly, more like different shapes, in sound. Triangles, circles, hexagrams, helixes and other shapes more complicated. The puzzle of it was, the Yeti language didn't have numbers and the Yeti couldn't, or chose not to, count other than by holding up their fingers. But it all seemed to work out perfectly well. The Yeti had their own way of doing things.

I'm beginning to catch on to it all, thought Fenn. He wanted to stay with the Yeti more than ever. He was just waiting for the right moment to ask. But now, the problem was how to get his spear to fly – not to flop – before the Spear Contest.

The contest was an even bigger event than Fenn had realised. It seemed Yeti lived throughout the Sanaskars, in valleys that trapped warm air currents. The Spear Contest was open to all. Visiting Yeti began to arrive the evening before. On the morning itself, they were streaming in, with baskets of food which they added to the feast already set out on the rocks.

The new arrivals spotted Fenn at once. They backed

off, afraid, until Arkon told of how he'd come to be there, and that the Most Ancient herself had permitted him to stay.

Everyone was here to enjoy themselves. Fenn was caught up in the festive mood. He was glad he hadn't opted out, that he was part of all this. He helped to mark out the contest ground with red lines made from a dye of pounded berries. Each marker represented a round in the contest between two teams. The winning team was whichever had the most contestants who'd been successful in the total number of rounds. Then, the best five from either side would compete to light the Spear Fire.

'What's happening now, Arkon?'

The Yeti were heading towards a row of baskets, filled with sticks, set out before the Most Ancient.

'We make our teams. Short sticks are a team together. Same with the long sticks.'

'I hope we're in the same team.'

Fenn reached into the basket. A short stick! And yes, Arkon chose a short stick too. The order of throw was by order of height, the smallest first.

'Look! He makes the start,' said Arkon.

A toddler, urged on by his parents, threw his self-made spear, a small stick, with gusto. It landed at his feet, but a burst of cheering brought a grin to his face and he clapped and cheered himself. Each contestant received the same enthusiastic applause, however short or long their throw.

'Now your turn, Yeti Boy,' said Arkon. 'You

remember what I have told you?'

'Take it slow. Take it easy. Take it steady.'

Whatever he did, thought Fenn, no one would jeer at him. But his stomach was doing somersaults as he went to the starting point. He didn't want to make a hash of it. Not just for himself and his team, but to show Arkon his patient hours of teaching hadn't been wasted.

Fenn focused his eye on the marker.

'Now, breathe in,' he murmured to himself.

As he breathed out, he let the spear fly.

The spear tippled over the first marker.

Claps, cheers!

Whew, so far so good!

Arkon gave him the thumbs up. Fenn ran to add a small pebble to the others in the pile for his team, which showed he'd made it through the first round.

'You do good, Yeti Boy. More better than me!' said Isa.

'But I'm bigger than you,' Fenn smiled down at her.

'You like being with the Yeti, yes?'

'You bet I do, Isa.'

'I like you here too.'

'But there's someone who doesn't. Ruala!'

Fenn didn't see much of her, which suited him fine. But now she was standing a few metres away. She was gripping her spear so tightly he could see the whites of her knuckles.

'Ruala wishes I wasn't here,' he said.

Isa nodded. 'That is so. It's because of her Happening.'

Before Fenn could ask anything further, the Most

Ancient gave a whistling, and the next round of the contest began.

Fenn made it through the next two rounds, but his spear failed to make it over the fourth marker. He'd done better than he'd expected. But their team was losing.

'It is early yet,' said Arkon.

As the contest progressed, the crowd became quiet. In the silence, the tension mounted. This was the last round. Fenn's team was three points behind. Arkon was still to throw, and on the other side, it was Burso and Ruala. Fenn watched as Ruala raised her spear, and effortlessly let it fly.

She's good, I have to give her that, he thought.

Now it was Arkon's turn. His spear flew over the marker, but their team was still two points behind. Burso's turn next. If he succeeded, his team would be the winner. He walked slowly to the starting point, as if he just happened to be walking there. How can Burso be so cool! thought Fenn. This was like a penalty shoot out; win or lose on a single kick.

The spear rose, arched, fell.

The triumphant Burso leapt into the air to a burst of cheers. Arkon bounded over and presented him with a slice of watermelon. Fenn noticed the losers were all giving the winning team something tasty to eat. He fetched a handful of the creepy-crawlies the Elders had roasted, and gave them to Cheb.

'Congratulations. I know you like these!'

Cheb tossed them into his mouth.

'You learn the Yeti way quick, Yeti Boy! Ah, here is Arkon. Now is the time, my friend, to see if you light the Spear Fire.'

Fenn gave the thumbs up. 'Good luck, Arkon.'

'Put your best thinking with me, Yeti Boy. I go now.'

Fenn watched after him as he joined the finalists. They each took a stick to determine the order of throw. This is the big time, he thought, as they lined up:

Glat

Jede

Burso

Arkon

Ruala.

Fenn was sure he could hear his heart beating aloud through the silence. It was obvious that cheering was out of order, but every bit of him was focused on Arkon, willing him to win.

Glat went to the starting point. He threw with force, and the spear landed well beyond the last marker, which Fenn had thought impossible to reach. Jede's spear fell just short of it. He shrugged and stood aside for Burso. Cool as before, Burso adjusted his balance. In a flowing movement, he let fly the spear. It fell a metre beyond Glat's throw. At that moment, Burso was in the lead.

Now, it was Arkon to throw.

'Go for it, Arkon!' Fenn whispered to himself.

Arkon took his time, adjusting the weight on his feet, the position of his shoulders. For some moments, he just stood, lost in himself. Then, the spear seemed to be lifting his hand, and took flight.

'Yes!' breathed Fenn.

His excitement was throbbing like a drum in every cell of his body. Arkon had won! Arkon would light the Spear Fire! Ruala would never be able to match him. But where was Ruala? She's chickened out, he thought. She knows she can't beat Arkon.

Then, there she was. She was striding towards the starting point. She looked fixedly in the distance as if at something she wanted to kill. Her face was set and hard. She wasn't like a Yeti, she was mean, thought Fenn. He knew he was being mean himself, but he hoped she'd mess up her throw so it wouldn't go beyond the first marker.

Ruala took her turn so quickly that the spear was in the air before he realised she'd thrown it. It sped, low and fast.

Fenn watched, anxiety rising like a storm inside him. He opened his mouth to bid the spear stop! There was a rush to see where it had landed. Ruala herself stayed where she was, as if now the spear was thrown, she had turned herself to stone.

Her spear, and Arkon's, lay a few metres apart, but their tips were level.

'What happens now?' asked Fenn. 'Do you have another go?'

Arkon shook his head.

'Then do you toss for it, to see who lights the fire?'

Again, Arkon shook his head.

'Arkon and Ruala, both, light the Spear Fire,' said the Most Ancient.

The spears, Fenn's amongst them, were already built into a pyramid. Two youngsters came forward, each holding a flaming torch. Arkon took the torch offered him. Ruala turned away, and went to walk off.

'Ruala!'

It was the Most Ancient who summoned her back. She paused. Looked at the ground. Grabbed at the torch. The Most Ancient gave the sign. Eyeing each other, Arkon and Ruala set their torches to the Spear Fire and it leapt into flame.

At once Ruala fled and this time no one tried to detain her.

Good riddance! thought Fenn. He ran to Arkon and thumped him on the back. 'You were brilliant! But what's wrong? Is it because you didn't win on your own? That doesn't matter—'

'No, not that.'

'Ruala! It's Ruala isn't it?'

Arkon gave a sudden shake of his shoulders as if to free himself of what had upset him.

'Look, Yeti Boy!'

He pointed towards the fire. Everyone had stood back except for the Elders. Earlier, Fenn had noticed, they had been pounding rocks of different colours to dust. It was Cheb's mother who threw in a handful first. Fenn heard a sizzling, then a fountain of green and pink sparks shot into the sky.

'Fireworks!' breathed Fenn.

Isa touched his arm. 'Good, yes?'

'Magic! It's magic, Isa.'

'And now the Spear Dance, Yeti Boy!'

The Yeti moved slowly as if swayed by a gentle breeze. The whistling grew louder. Their steps quickened. Fenn had always thought dancing was a girly, wimpy thing. But Arkon was no wimp. Nor were Burso and Cheb. And they were dancing! Even the Most Ancient had joined the circle that was weaving around the Spear Fire.

Isa called him, and made a space beside her for Fenn. His feet stamped out the beat. His body was moving this way and that, free-flowing like water. He joined the whistling, adding notes of his own.

I can't believe this is me! A surge of happiness swept over him.

Later, in his sleep, Fenn smiled.

But Arkon couldn't sleep. He tossed and turned and finally got up, went out and stood by the Spear Fire. He looked into the dying embers. He knew what he must do:

He must tell Yeti Boy about Ruala.

Not now, but soon.

His Knowing would tell him when it was the time.

8.

A few days after the Spear Contest, Fenn and Arkon were collecting firewood. They began to make a neat stack of it, ready to take home later.

'That will do for now. Let us sit down,' said Arkon.

Fenn added a few twigs to the stack, then stretched out on the grass. The trees made a dappled shelter from the sun.

'It's a good place, this. I always like coming here.'

To make himself more comfortable, Fenn sorted out wood to lean against. He offered some to Arkon who brushed it aside.

Arkon sat stiff and upright, his eyes narrowed, as if peering through the dark to see what was beyond.

'What are you thinking about, Arkon?'

'I am thinking about Ruala.'

'Ruala!'

'Please, don't start up, Yeti Boy.'

But Fenn was already seething. 'I haven't forgotten that carry-on at the Spear Contest! Ruala almost spoilt it – for you, Arkon, most of all.'

Fenn hurled away the twig that had been sticking into him. He watched with satisfaction as it landed in a prickly bush. 'If Ruala tries her tantrums and sulks on me again, I'm going to tell her where to get off.'

'No, no, Yeti Boy!' protested Arkon, in such agitation Fenn was taken aback.

That was Ruala for you, Fenn thought. Trouble, even when she wasn't there. 'Let's leave it, Arkon. Don't let's talk about her.'

'I must, Yeti Boy.' Arkon gave a look, pleading with him not to argue.

Fenn hadn't a clue what was going on, but he could see it was upsetting Arkon. 'Okay, I'm listening,' he said. 'What *is* this, about Ruala?'

Arkon stared at the ground. A frown creased deep in his forehead. He'd tried to prepare himself... but where to begin? He didn't *want* to begin at all. Already, it was hurting, remembering back. But he must tell Fenn, it was exactly the time.

A butterfly landed on the grass. Arkon watched it, sunning itself. After a few moments, the butterfly flitted off. So bright! So happy! Like Joz, he thought, and his face lit up.

'To begin, Yeti Boy, I shall tell you about Joz.'

'Joz?' Fenn couldn't place the name. 'Who is Joz?'

'Before, Joz is my best friend.' Arkon gave a lively whistling. 'That is Joz for you,' he laughed. 'Always up to something or other. He has very quick thinking, you know. More quick than this Yeti, I tell him!'

'But what's Joz got to do with Ruala?'

'Ruala, she is the sister of Joz. Before, Ruala is my friend too.' Arkon's face shadowed over, all the laughter gone. 'Before,' he sighed, 'we are happy together – Ruala and Arkon and Joz.'

Before what? puzzled Fenn. Then he shivered. But it wasn't from cold. He knew this feeling – a chill foreboding that wouldn't be shaken off. He was very tense and silent as he waited for Arkon to go on.

Arkon spoke more to himself now, with his gaze focused into the distance:

'Every big sunaround, Joz and Ruala go to visit friends who live quite far away.'

Fenn listened, without interrupting.

Later, when Arkon had finished, Fenn went over it all in his mind. He hoped that what Arkon had told him wasn't true, but deep down inside he knew it must be.

On the morning that Joz and Ruala had set off to visit their friends, Arkon was up before them. He caught a fish and cooked it. They shared the fish together.

'When we get back, I'll cook one for you,' said Joz.

'With apricots! They'll be ripe then,' said Ruala.

Arkon licked his lips. 'Hurry! I can't wait! Go now and come back quick.

Joz and Ruala always took the same route. They had their favourite places to stop to gather food and shelter at night. They hadn't much further to go when they saw an outcrop of small blue berries higher up the mountain. These berries didn't grow in their valley, and they climbed up to get some. Then, further up, they caught sight of a waterfall where a mountain stream tumbled over a sheer drop of rock.

'Let's go cool off. I'm as hot as a roasting fire!' said Joz.

It looked an easy climb up but each time they thought they were almost there, another outcrop of rock blocked their way. It began to get dark. But the night was warm, and they were used to sleeping out. The next morning, however, a mist surrounded them. They would have to wait till it cleared.

At last they began to make their way back to connect with their path.

'Ruala!' Joz motioned her back. But too late. Two human men rounded the rock just ahead.

'Ruala, run!'

She raced over the flat expanse of grass, and scrambled on up between the rocks. Her brother's whistling was like an arrow speeding her on, and she thought he was close behind her till she realised she couldn't hear his footfall. She turned to see where he was. Joz was standing at the base of the rock, his arms held wide, blocking the way between the men and herself. The tallest of the men raised what looked like a small branch stripped of leaves but she knew it held danger.

'Joz, watch out!'

There was a crack like a rock splitting and a fiery flash, like lightning. Blood spurted from Joz's right shoulder and his left leg, between the knee and ankle. He gave a whistling that was an order to her, and a desperate plea, telling her to flee.

'I'm not leaving you, Joz!'

The man next to him pointed the thing that had wounded her brother towards her. She dodged just in time to miss being struck, and lost herself in a maze of boulders higher up. The men gave chase but she was too fast for them.

Ruala crouched, with her face cupped in her hands. Tears streamed through her fingers. But she must help Joz. She edged round from her hiding place and looked down.

She had a clear view of the men. The smaller had no hair on his greasy head. His face looked sour, like an unripe plum. The other was sharp-featured, and looked like a hawk. Hawk Face and Bald Head stood on either side of her brother. Already they had tied his arms behind his back. Hawk Face began to tie a rope round Joz's neck, which Bald Head held at the other end, all the time jumping about, as if fleas were biting his feet.

He was laughing. 'We found ourselves a Yeti! We're rich! We came looking for silver and diamonds in these here hills! But a real live Yeti! It's as good as finding a Martian! All over the world they'll be queuing up for a sight of him! We'll just sit back and watch the money roll in.'

Hawk Face tightened the knot around Joz. 'The sooner we get on the move, the better.'

'What about the other one? One Yeti is good. Two is better.'

'Don't reckon it's hung about. Let's get this one down. Then, we come back for the other.'

They stared down at Joz.

'How are we going to move it?'

'It can walk. It's not hurt too badly. Up you get, you hairy brute!'

They hauled Joz to his feet.

'Let me go or you will die.'

Startled, the men looked about them, then at each other.

'What did you say?' they exploded.

'Nothing, I didn't say anything,' each protested, one to the other.

'Let me go or you will die,' Joz said again.

'It's the Yeti!' stammered Bald Head. ''The brute's talking jibber-jabber, but I thought it said—"

'Me too.' Hawk Face looked nervous. 'The locals say they can talk, and get into your head so you can twig what they're saying, and they can understand you.'

'*I'm* not being spooked by a Yeti.'

Bald Head booted Joz in the stomach.

'Another jibber-jabber out of you and there's more where that came from. Now, let's get moving.'

He tugged at the rope round Joz's neck.

'Let me go or you will die,' Joz said a third time, followed by a whistling that was filled with menace and warning.

'No, Joz! No!' whispered Ruala. She realised what her

brother was going to do. She must stop him. She began to clamber down from her hiding place. A scattering of falling stones gave her away.

Hawk Face saw her first. 'Give me the gun! We can get that one too!'

'Ruala, stand back! Ruala!'

Joz's voice calling her name was the last thing she heard before his whistling. The whistling was so high she heard it in her head rather than as an actual sound. There was nothing she could do to stop what would follow. She stood, not caring what became of her, as an avalanche of rock and earth thundered down and around.

When all was silent at last, she found herself on the edge of a crevice that dipped endlessly into gloomy depths.

'Joz,' she murmured. But she did not expect him to answer. He had caused the rock-fall. He knew he would be killed in it, and the Humans too. He had meant it to happen.

Later Ruala turned back for home. Her face was like ash. Her eyes stared as if she had gone from her body to somewhere else.

The first person she saw was Arkon. He realised at once something terrible had occurred.

'When she tells me about Joz,' said Arkon to Fenn, 'her voice is all on one note. But after, it is like she has a tornado whirling about inside. She says the same things over and over, she cannot be still. The Most Ancient sends her to sleep with a whistling. When she wakes, Ruala is quieter but she is not as she was before.'

'No, she wouldn't be,' Fenn whispered. His chest was tight with feelings, all of them hurting so much he could hardly breathe. He tried to take in what Arkon had told him. Fenn wanted to say, not all humans are like those men, but he couldn't. He knew if they had taken Joz he'd be put on show, like a freak, and that wouldn't be the end of it. People would come to the Sanaskars on a Yeti hunt, not just those in it for the money, but scientists eager to study them. The next thing, there'd be package tours, tourists coming to gawp at them. The Yeti wouldn't be able to stop it. The Most Ancient was right; if humans and Yeti came together, it would be the end of the Yeti way. The wonder of it was, they had let him stay. He understood why Ruala hated him.

'I'd hate all humans too if I was her,' he burst out. 'But why does she hate you, Arkon?' Fenn answered for himself. 'Because you saved me, of course, and I'm a human. I'm sorry, Arkon, I'm really sorry.'

'For why do they do that to Joz, Yeti Boy?'

Fenn was struggling not to cry. 'I don't know Arkon. Humans do things like that to each other, too.'

'Maybe Humans don't feel hurt like a Yeti, that is the for why of how they can do it,' said Arkon.

'Whatever it is, I'm ashamed to be a human.' Fenn spoke with such force, he trembled. 'It was humans who killed your best friend – or as good as.'

'That was not of your doing, Yeti Boy.'

'But it's because of me that Ruala hates you!'

Then Fenn asked the question that lurked in his mind: 'If you had another chance, Arkon, would you leave me on that ledge? I wouldn't blame you one bit if you said yes.'

'A Happening is what it is. I cannot make it *not* happen. I never go thinking of that, Yeti Boy.'

A breeze drifted in through the trees. The grass shifted, weaving patterns. Fenn and Arkon watched with concentrated attention, not knowing what to say to each other.

'We are upset, Yeti Boy, you and me both,' said Arkon at last.

'It's all so horrible,' said Fenn. 'And to think I planned to have a go at Ruala! Thank goodness you told me all this.'

'I was not wanting to,' Arkon admitted. 'But we are friends.' He gave the start of a smile. 'The way of it is, we share the good and the not good, and we're still friends after, yes!'

Arkon flexed his shoulders as if a burden had lifted from them. 'Now,' he said, rising to his feet and pulling up Fenn at the same time. 'What about this wood, Yeti Boy?'

'What about it?' Fenn asked, eager to change the subject.

'We must be deciding. Do we take the wood home?'

'Or leave it till later?' quizzed Fenn.

They looked each other.

Picked up the wood, without a word spoken.

And carried it back to the cave.

9.

'Arkon, where are you? Have any of you seen Arkon?'

It was Isa. She hurried to where Fenn was chatting to Burso and Cheb. The three stood by a very prickly bush.

'We've been taking it in turns to jump over it,' said Fenn. 'I don't know where Arkon's got to,' he added.

'The Most Ancient has sent me to fetch him— oh, there's Arkon. I shall leave you to your prickles!'

'What could the Most Ancient want?' frowned Fenn. 'She hasn't sent for Arkon before, not since I've been here, anyway.'

'Ask Cheb, Yeti Boy. His nose is twitching! He is sniffing it out.'

'I'll leave that to you, Burso. Watch this!' Cheb took a

leap over the bush. But the game had lost its allure. Impatiently they waited for Arkon to return.

As soon as they saw him, 'What did the Most Ancient want?' they chorused.

'Tell us,' urged Burso. 'Cheb is popping his guts, he's so longing to know!'

Quickly, Arkon told them.

'Is this for real, Arkon?' asked Fenn. 'We're going to the Keepers? And then for a wander-about?'

'We go this very now. I am to take you. The Most Ancient tells me herself. It's good news, yes?'

'It's mind-blowingly brilliant!' said Fenn. 'Off to the Keepers and a wander-about! Yes, oh yes!' he whooped. He'd been pleading with Arkon to take him, but had always been fobbed off. Now, suddenly, they were going. It must mean the Yeti have accepted me, Fenn smiled to himself. When he got back, that would be the time to ask if he could stay with them forever.

But now to get ready. Not that it would take long. He'd just take his backpack and the bottle he'd brought with him, for water.

The water bottle was proving to be a fascinating attraction for Cheb and Burso, and the others who'd come to see them off. Till now, no one had shown any interest in Fenn's clothes or anything he had brought with him. They seemed to regard his clothes as part of him, skins that he put on and off when he wanted. But the plastic water bottle intrigued them.

Cheb held it up to the sun and peered through the plastic.

'What tree is it made of, Yeti Boy?'

'Plastic's not made out of a tree. I'm not sure what it is made of, exactly. I didn't make it myself.'

'The same as you don't catch your own fish!' said Burso.

'All right, all right, don't go on! But I nearly caught one! I had it in my hands, but it slid away at the last moment.'

'Yes, and frogs fall out of the sky! We've heard that before, Yeti Boy. Here, catch.' Cheb tossed him the water bottle. Fenn caught it one-handed. 'It's just the fish that get away!' he grinned.

But what was the matter with Isa? She was standing apart from the others. Her shoulders drooped, her mouth was turned down. He went over and knelt down beside her.

'What is it, Isa?'

'I am happy that you will be with the Keepers but I am sad, too, that you are going. When I am big,' she sniffled, 'I will hold the sad and the happy inside me together. But now, I'm too small.' She broke off, and burst into tears.

'Don't cry, Isa. I'll be back.'

'I'm wanting to come with you,' she said. 'But it's not the time for me to go to the Keepers. I'll miss you, Yeti Boy.'

'I'll miss you too, Isa. But what's this?'

She held out a large, luscious peach. 'It is for you. I want you to plant the stone for me.'

'You mean, you want me to plant it here?'

'No, no, you must find the place that's right for it.

Then, when you come back, you shall tell me where it is. I'll watch over it, and when it's a tree I shall say to myself, "Yeti Boy made it grow here for Isa." Will you do that?'

'Plant the peach stone? Of course! Of course I will.'

Isa brushed off her tears, and smiled. 'Now my sadness is gone. Thank you, Yeti Boy.'

'Do I get a peach too?' asked Arkon.

'No,' Isa said firmly. 'Only Yeti Boy has a peach. But I'll miss you too!' She reached up and hugged him. 'Tell the Keepers, from Isa, that from here –' she put her hand on her heart – 'I send them bright wishes.'

'I'll tell them, little Isa. Now, we go. Are you ready, Yeti Boy?'

'Am I ever!' Fenn replied, with a whistling to show that he couldn't wait to get on the move.

When he looked back, he saw Isa, sitting on Burso's broad shoulders, together with Cheb and the others. They were waving.

'See you soon!'

Fenn was looking forward to the trip, his first trip away from the valley. It was an adventure. But it gave him a good feeling to know that he had so many friends when he returned.

Arkon looked over his shoulder to check that Fenn was keeping up with him. Fenn was finding it hard, but trying not to show it.

Arkon slowed down, and waited for him to catch up. The visit to the Keepers had been as much of a surprise to him as to Fenn. It was even more surprising that it was the Most Ancient who had suggested it. She had sent Isa to fetch him, and he had scarcely seated himself on the mat before her when she came at once to the point.

'I wish for Fenn to meet with the Keepers. Will you take him?' she had asked.

'Yes, yes!' beamed Arkon. 'He is wanting to go. I am thinking you wouldn't allow it, that he must stay here.'

The Most Ancient smiled. 'The Keepers are not so far away. They know Fenn is with us, of course. We are agreed it is to the good that he should be with them for just a little.'

It did not occur to Arkon to question why. That the Most Ancient had told him so was enough.

'So tell me, how do you find the boy, Arkon?'

'He isn't like those Humans who tried to take Joz!' Arkon wanted the Most Ancient to know that. Then he realised she would know already or she would never have allowed Fenn to stay. Flustered, he began to apologise.

'No, no,' she said. 'I'm interested to hear your thinking. You have told him about Joz, yes, just before?'

'He was angry with Ruala, so I told him. Fenn is not angry with Ruala now. He is ashamed for the Humans. 'I do not know how Human live at all,' Arkon burst out. 'Fenn can't light a fire to warm himself. He can't catch himself a fish to eat.' In his eagerness to share what he'd discovered he edged closer to the Most Ancient. 'Not only that, he doesn't have the Knowing. Without our

78

Knowing, soon there would be no Yeti!'

'Fenn has it, he has the Knowing,' said the Most Ancient.

Arkon frowned, perplexed. 'But he can't tell which path leads to where, which roots or whatever are good-eaters and which will put poison in his stomach—' He broke off. 'But if you say he has the Knowing, Most Ancient, then he must have it. Maybe the Elders haven't learnt him how to use it like all the other things they've not learnt him.'

'Then you learn him, the way we learn the little ones. You will see, Fenn has the Knowing.' The Most Ancient laughed, seeing that Arkon was struggling to be convinced. 'Already you have learnt the boy much. You have taken good care of him. I am pleased.'

Her praise gave Arkon the courage to ask what he hadn't dared ask so far. 'After the Keepers, can I take Fenn on a wander-about? He is wanting to go, to be like a Yeti.'

'But Fenn is not a Yeti,' the Most Ancient reminded him. 'You may take him on a wander-about. But you will both be here when it is the time for him to return to the Humans.' Her voice held a edge of warning. 'He must go, Arkon.'

Arkon lowered his head. He had hoped, just a little, that Fenn would be able to stay. 'I wouldn't have asked,' he said.

The Most Ancient nodded, approving. 'It is not our way to ask for what cannot be.'

From wherever he was, Arkon could tell from the sun's position in the sky when it would rise over the White

Bark Tree. He never looked to check, as if by not looking he would stop the sun's progress. He knew that Fenn never looked at the tree either. He didn't want to think about him leaving. Yeti Boy is here, in the now, he told himself. He would think only of that. And he must do as the Most Ancient had instructed. But he'd seen no sign that Fenn had the Knowing, and wasn't looking forward to it.

Without much enthusiasm, Arkon searched about and picked some berries, a yellow, a red, and a blue one.

'Yeti Boy, tell me, which berries is good to eat. And which will make you—' He made as if to throw up. 'Or die,' he added.

'Arkon, how would I know? I've never seen them before.'

'Never mind about that, choose the good-eater.'

'What is this? Some sort of game? Oh all right, if you insist.'

Fenn chose the yellow berry.

Arkon popped it into his mouth. 'Mmm! You choose the good-eater.'

'It was a fluke. Just a guess. No big deal.'

Arkon walked on, picking a leaf here and there and more berries. Again he asked Fenn to tell him which were safe to eat.

Fenn flushed, annoyed. He was getting fed up with Arkon telling him what to do. 'What is all this? You know I can't tell you. Even in the place I come from I don't know what wild-growing things you can eat.

You're just trying to show me up.'

'I am trying to learn you,' said Arkon weightily. 'You're harder to learn than the little ones.' He gestured to things he'd set out. 'Look at each one. Ask to yourself, is it good to eat? Your Knowing will tell you Yes or No.'

'Oh, it's as easy as that, is it!'

'Yes,' replied Arkon firmly.

'I'm not a Yeti, remember,' Fenn retorted. 'I haven't got this Knowing as you call it. I haven't a clue what it is.'

'The Most Ancient says you have it, so you have,' Arkon flashed back.

That threw Fenn.

'Did the Most Ancient really say that?'

'You think I tell you what is not?'

Arkon glared, and Fenn backed off.

'Okay, okay! I'll give it a go. But don't expect any results.'

To his surprise, many of his choices turned out to be correct.

'For a start, you do well,' said Arkon. 'Until we get to the Keepers we eat only the good-eaters you choose.'

Fenn's mouth dropped. 'You've got be joking! We'll starve.'

Arkon shrugged. 'Okay, as you say, so we starve!' There was more to come. 'Now, which is the way to the Keepers? Do we cross the stream again or what? Ask your Knowing, Yeti Boy.'

'I thought this trip was going to be fun. It's more

like an exam with impossible questions,' muttered Fenn. He'd had enough. 'I give up. You tell me.'

Arkon sat down on a log on the stream's bank. 'No, you tell me.'

Fenn sighed. With Arkon in this mood, he'd more chance of moving the Sanaskar Mountains than getting him to budge till he'd done as he wanted. May as well get it over with. He glanced ahead to where a natural path formed itself along the bank of the stream. Another path led off it, through tall-growing grass. On the other side, the bank was overgrown with bushes. He knew, suddenly absolutely knew, which way they should take to the Keepers. Like he knew – or thought he did – that the plane would crash.

Without a word, Fenn waded into the shallows of the stream.

Arkon waded in after him. 'You've got good Knowing, Yeti Boy. But you must remember always to use it. It's easy to forget when you get in a fluster.'

'Do you think that's how Joz and Ruala got lost? I can imagine me doing that.' Fenn paused, with a troubled look. 'This Knowing you talk about, Arkon, can it tell you things besides what you can eat and which direction to go in?'

'It can tell you many things. But like for what?'

'Nothing. Forget it!' said Fenn. The ground had now cleared. 'Race you to the tree! The one with the big floppy flowers.' He was smaller and lighter than Arkon. He was sure he could beat him.

No such luck!

'I am bigger than you, and stronger, and faster, Yeti Boy!' grinned Arkon as he leant against the tree, not even puffed.

'Certainly your head is lots bigger,' Fenn grinned back at him. 'Now, if you want me to tell you the way to the Keepers... My Knowing says it's thataway. Am I right?'

'Now, whose head is blowing up, Yeti Boy!'

Arkon gave a whistling that made them both laugh. A startled bird watched after them, from its nest by the stream, as Fenn and Arkon, still laughing, went on their way to the Keepers.

10.

Kate looked up at the sky. It was grey and overcast. The clouds promised rain, or drizzle – a relentless drizzle that was more depressing than a heavy downpour. The summer wasn't over, but the damp was seeping into her bones.

She checked to see that she had all she needed for the day's work. The others in the group had suggested she leave it to them, but she was glad to be occupied with the work she loved. The worst moments came when her mind was too exhausted to think, and then her feelings would take over, and she'd be left with the torment and anguish that as yet there was no news of Fenn.

As the days passed, the possibility of finding him alive was increasingly remote, she knew that. She was one who dealt in facts. But despite the facts that suggested otherwise, she couldn't bring herself to believe that Fenn was dead. She knew the rest of the group had given up hope, but were too tactful to tell her. They were at a loss as to how to deal with her, and were uneasy in her presence.

Not so, Hubbert!

But then, Hubbert was as thick-skinned as a rhino.

However, when he was away with the search parties, she found it more difficult to keep herself together. Keeping Hubbert in his place consumed her energy, and diverted her thoughts and fears about Fenn. But she suspected there was something he was keeping from her. She was certain of it when she heard him talking to a rough-looking couple who came to the camp. They were English or American, in their late twenties she guessed, and both had drug-hazed eyes.

They were asking Hubbert about the Yeti.

'We heard there's one been spotted hereabouts.'

'Yeti?' laughed Hubbert. 'Dream on! It's just talk. You should know better than to believe that sort of rubbish.'

'Yeah? But what about this footprint then? The locals are all babbling on about it.'

Hubbert glanced down at his boots.

'You mean… Hey, man! Crazy! These locals will tell you anything! So, what's the deal on this kid that's gone missing?'

Hubbert couldn't let any possibility slip by, but he had to make an effort to keep his fists at his side.

'Let's say it'll be worth your while.'

The man gave a twisted smile. 'Alive or dead, is it?'

'Clear off. Go on, off!'

'Okay, man, take it easy.'

Kate waited till they had gone.

'You're a liar, Hubbert, one way or the other. You told me something quite different about that footprint.'

'Yes, I told you the truth, Kate. I've come across those scum before. When they're not drugged, they hunt the wildlife to sell on to those types who fancy a tusked head over the mantelpiece or a bearskin on the floor.'

'Most of all,' burst in Tishaw, 'they hope to hunt the snow leopard to fetch the best price.' He grinned as he imitated Hubbert. 'Dream on!' he said. 'In all my life, I have not seen one.'

'If they found a Yeti, God knows what they'd do. Kill and skin it, I dare say, to make a quick buck. Another of their scams is selling bogus maps to oddballs who believe the stories about ancient cities in the Sanaskars, knee-deep in diamonds and gold.'

'Yes, I've heard some of those,' said Kate.

'I tell you, I'd do more than lie to rid the Sanaskars of those two. If I'd had my gun handy... Just joking,' Hubbert added, seeing the look on her face.

'I'm going back to work. You'll let me know if...' Her voice broke, and she ran quickly off.

'Missy is all in pieces. It's better for her to know about Fenn, one way or the other.'

'We'll up the reward, Tishaw. Maybe that will do it. And if we get any more Yeti hunters snooping about—'

'You leave them to me, Mr Hubbert.'

'In the meantime, we keep looking for Fenn. It puzzles me that we've found no further trace of him. But we will find him. He's there, somewhere. But where?' Hubbert looked up at the mountains, willing them to yield him an answer.

11.

Not far to the Keepers now, thought Fenn. Arkon had told him they'd be there by sunset. But the afternoon was drawing in, and Fenn wondered if Arkon had meant this small sunaround or the next. The trees had thinned out. They were walking across a wilderness of scrubland. No one could live here, he thought.

The hard ground suddenly turned soft and soggy. His feet squelched into it, and something grey and clammy oozed from between his toes. It was clay. They plodded on, sucking out their feet with each step.

'Look at this, Arkon.'

Fenn scooped up a handful of clay, squeezed the water out, and flattened it in his palm. He stuck a twig through it and held it over his head.

'It's to keep off the sun!'

Arkon sighed. 'You're as mad as a mad monkey, Yeti Boy. I hope you'll not be behaving like that for the Keepers.'

So far, Fenn knew the Keepers made the Happenings, but he hadn't been able to discover anything further. 'Tell me about them. What are they like?'

'You begin to know already. Isa is a Keeper.'

'Isa! A Keeper!' gasped Fenn.

'Later, she will live with the other Keepers, where we go now,' said Arkon. 'But you must notice already, Isa isn't quite the same as the other little ones. We know from when she draws the star!'

'Draws the star? How do you mean?'

Fenn expected he'd have to batter Arkon with questions, but for once he was eager to explain.

'When a Yeti is this many big sunarounds,' Arkon held up three fingers, 'the Keepers come to visit. They bring presents, fruit and honey and toys made of wood. They play with the little ones. Then, as if it is another game, the Keepers clear a patch of ground, stamp it hard and flat, and throw a light scattering of earth over it. Next, they give the little ones a stick and say, "Draw whatever you want."'

Arkon paused to check their direction.

'Mostly,' he went on, 'the little ones draw a squiggle. But a few sometimes, they draw a star. Perfect! Exact! I saw Isa do it.'

'That's amazing!'

Even with a ruler and compass, Fenn couldn't get the angles accurate and the star points even.

'The Keepers have the most true Knowing. You are lucky, Yeti Boy, that Isa takes a liking to you at the beginning. It is a sign to the others that though you are Human, you bring no harm. It is for why they let you stay.'

'All the time I've spent with Isa, and she's never mentioned it!'

'Of course not! The Keepers don't make a show of themselves. It's not their way. Not like this Yeti!' said Arkon, thumping his chest.

Fenn thumped his own chest too. 'Not like this Yeti Boy either!'

'It is not only because of Isa that you stay,' went on Arkon, as if he'd just remembered. 'The Most Ancient is a Keeper also.'

'Now you tell me!' Fenn protested, indignant. 'No one tells me anything!'

'I tell you if you ask, Yeti Boy.'

'I'm always asking you questions but you never answer them, Arkon. You know you don't.'

'That's because you don't ask good questions,' he said smugly. 'The Most Ancient is always a Keeper. When the last dies, another comes to live with us. When the time comes, Isa will be our Most Ancient.'

Fenn looked at him wistfully. 'It's all brilliant. You're lucky to be born a Yeti. It's better than being a human, I can tell you.'

He remembered what the Most Ancient had said, about wanting to be what you were not. Not all the wanting in the world could make him a Yeti. But he was Yeti Boy, and that was the next best thing.

After what Arkon had told him, Fenn was even more curious to meet the Keepers. But it seemed they'd reached a dead end. They were approaching the bare flank of a mountain, a sheer rise of rock. At its base was a scattering of large boulders. Arkon disappeared behind them. Fenn peered round. No sign of him. There was a gap in the rock-face but it was too dark to see in. With relief, he heard Arkon's whistling, urging him to follow. He wished Arkon had waited. Fenn had to make an effort to still the panic at not being able to see what was underfoot or where he was going. Using his hands to steady himself, he eased his way forward. His eyes involuntarily closed, as if to sharpen his sense of hearing and touch.

He felt the sun on his face before he saw it.

His eyes flashed open.

'Good eh?' beamed Arkon.

'Yes, oh yes!' said Fenn.

Before him were soft rolling pastures. Mountains rose up around, but here everything seemed to sparkle, the flowers, the grass, the stream and the fish!

So many fish!

'We take some for the Keepers,' said Arkon. He lay flat on the grassy bank. Suddenly he reached out. He grabbed, and leapt up, clasping a silver-scaled fish. He stunned it quickly with the side of his hand, then struck it with a small rock. He caught ten or so more, and killed them in the same expert way.

'Now you, Yeti Boy. Catch a fish to take to the Keepers. Always, we take fish when we visit.'

Even *he* should be able to catch a fish here, thought Fenn, but he hesitated. He'd seen Arkon catch and kill fish many times, of course, but never so many one after the other, and always, he realised, he looked away when it came to killing them.

'What is it, Yeti Boy?'

'Nothing,' said Fenn. He must do it, if only just once. He lay down on the bank beside Arkon. There were so many fish, he was spoilt for choice.

'Got one.'

He killed it as Arkon had done.

'Good,' said Arkon. 'You catch your fish, and kill it, the Yeti way.'

Fenn was proud that he'd caught a fish at last, and sad, too, at the killing. But he didn't regret it. It was something he knew he had to do, and he'd done it. They wrapped the fish in leaves from the fig tree growing nearby. Fenn hoped they didn't have to go much further, or the fish would start to stink.

'We are here already,' said Arkon. He gave the whistling he used for his own name, then the whistling he used for Fenn's. In reply came a whistling that was high and finely pitched. Arkon recognised it at once. He hadn't expected this!

'We are mighty lucky, Yeti Boy. Look who comes to meet us. Of all the Keepers, he is the most special!'

Fenn saw a tall figure striding towards them. He was the tallest Yeti that Fenn had seen so far. His limbs were long and slender. He stood almost straight, more in the Human than the Yeti way.

He embraced Arkon, then he turned to Fenn.

'Welcome, Fenn, Yeti Boy. I am Thes.'

He's awesome, thought Fenn, but *awesome*! He'd never met a king or anyone royal, but that's what Thes made him think of. He was glad he'd not arrived empty-handed.

He offered the fish.

'For you, Sir,' he said. 'It's fresh, I just caught it.'

Thes bowed. 'You are most kind.'

That was the moment Fenn's tummy chose to give a desperate rumble. He went red, but for all his royal presence, Thes was amused.

'We shall eat, and soon.'

They were heading towards what Fenn took to be a cave. On approaching the entrance, he saw it was actually a tunnel with a high ceiling. It was dusk now, but the tunnel was brightly lit. This was a soft clear light, like the halogen lamp on his bedside table in England. But the Yeti couldn't have invented such an advanced form of electric light.

'Where's the light coming from?' he asked.

'It is here,' said Thes.

He hadn't understood the question, Fenn thought. 'Yes, but what's making it?'

'He is all questions, this Yeti Boy.' Arkon shot Fenn a warning look not to trouble Thes further.

Thes smiled, however. 'As this is always beneath us,' he said, tapping at the ground with his foot. 'So, too, the light is always around us.'

Fenn realised that this was all the answer he was going to get. He stared at the rock, seeking a further clue. It must have something luminous in it, he decided. It was the only explanation he could think of.

The light ahead was coming from an unmistakable source. A fire lit up a circle of grass that was open to the sky. Bustling about were fifteen or so Yeti, tall and slender like Thes, though he was the tallest of all. Tending the fire were two girls and two boys, a few years older than Fenn, he guessed.

'Arkon!'

They came running, hugged Arkon, and bombarded him with questions about their families and friends. At the sight of Fenn, they fell silent and drew back, waiting till Thes beckoned them forward to be introduced. They each gave their names and a whistling with it.

'Now, let's eat,' said Thes.

Already, green peppers and carrots with sweet smelling herbs were roasting over red glowing chunks of wood. Fenn gripped his tummy to stop it rumbling. They'd eaten only the good-eaters he'd chosen, Arkon had kept him to that, and this would be the first decent hot food he'd eaten since they'd set out. The young Keepers seemed in charge of the cooking. They cleaned the fish and set to roasting them, stuffed with walnuts and peaches. The food was delicious. Fenn wondered if he'd eaten the fish that he had caught, but decided not to dwell on it.

They stayed by the fire as the night drew in. The moon rose up. It revealed the outline of the mountain around them – it was as if they were sitting in the heart of it. A young Keeper set up a whistling, smooth and velvety. Fenn's eyes began to close. He willed them open. There was something extraordinary about this place. While he was here, he wanted to make the most of every moment.

12.

Fenn woke the next morning in a rock-walled room. At least, he thought it was morning. There was no natural light to go by. The room was lit in the same mysterious way as the tunnel. He inspected the walls, and the floor, and the ceiling also, but they gave no clue as to where the light came from.

He went over and prodded the lump under the goatskin, and jumped as Arkon leapt up.

'I thought you were asleep!'

'You thought wrong, Yeti Boy. I am waiting for you to wake up.'

'Oh yes!' laughed Fenn. 'Can we look round?'

'Thes will take you, you will be with Thes.'

'You mean, just me on my own?'

'Why such a face? Thes is like the highest peak of a wonderful mountain.'

'Yes, but I'd feel better if you came along too.'

'Do you think Thes is going to eat you? Like you thought I was going to, when I found you?' Arkon chomped his jaws and licked his lips.

'I never really thought you were going to eat me! Well, only for a moment.'

'Look, if you don't want Thes to show you around, Yeti Boy, you tell him yourself. Also, you tell him yourself if you don't want him to make your Happening.'

'Thes? Is he going to make me a Happening?'

Arkon nodded. 'But only if you want. You decide later. Now, we eat.'

The young Keepers had breakfast set out in the same place as they'd eaten the previous night. Before them was fruit – peaches and cherries – sweetcorn, and water in cups of polished wood.

Soon after, Thes arrived. He didn't eat anything and Fenn felt uneasy eating in his presence.

'You must eat all you need to take your hunger away,' Thes told him. 'I will eat later. When you are ready, I will show you the Place of Many Happenings.'

Fenn got quickly to his feet, careful not to look at Arkon, who started chomping his jaws to the amusement of the young Keepers.

Thes led the way from one rock-lined corridor to another. At last they came to a circular high-roofed

cavern. On the ceiling and on the floor beneath was a five-pointed star. The lines and angles and points were carved with immaculate precision. A well-lit hall faced them. It stretched on endlessly, forking off now and then to others. The walls were hung with silver engravings, like Arkon's.

'You may look,' said Thes, smiling at Fenn's anxiety about whether he was allowed to or not.

The engravings were expertly done. Some had an extra quality that captured not only what the Yeti looked like, but also their feelings. Most of them showed everyday things. In one, a middle-aged Yeti sat on a rock, gazing up at a star-studded sky. In another, a young Yeti female stood outside a cave, clasping a clay pot filled with peaches; perhaps a gift from someone precious, Fenn thought.

'What's this one?' he ventured.

It showed a handsome young Yeti kneeling by a fire, gazing intently into the flames that leapt high.

'He says goodbye to his wife,' replied Thes.

'You mean, she died?'

Thes nodded.

Fenn picked out a few similar engravings, but not many Yeti, it seemed, wanted to have their sad Happenings recorded.

'When did the Keepers start making the Happenings?'

'Long ago, way back,' said Thes. 'I shall make your Happening, if you wish?'

'Yes, please.'

Fenn wasn't sure what he was letting himself in for, but he was excited that he was about to discover how the Happenings were made.

He followed Thes down yet another corridor. He wondered how many halls, caverns and linking corridors were set in the mountain. He was sure the Yeti couldn't have made them; they were another amazing natural feature. The Kate woman would go barmy over all this. Fenn shook his head to get her out of his mind. He hadn't thought of her since – he couldn't remember. He wasn't going to start now.

Thes was walking with a smooth, swift stride.

'It is here that I make your Happening,' he said.

He stood aside, and Fenn walked into the room beyond.

The room was circular, but it wasn't that which gripped his attention. The walls, floor and ceiling were perfectly smooth and silvery, like the Happenings the Keepers made. Set in the walls were rectangular gaps, about twenty centimetres long – how deep they were he couldn't tell. Carved into the floor, and set in gold, was a five-pointed star. Its centre sparkled, shone, glittered.

'Diamonds, they're diamonds,' breathed Fenn.

A young Keeper with very blue eyes came in, laid goatskins on either side of the diamond-studded circle, then left silently.

Thes indicated that Fenn should sit, then sat opposite, so they faced each other.

The goatskins seemed somehow out of place; rough

and crude compared with the smooth surfaces that looked ultra modern, Fenn thought. But Fenn was glad of their softness.

Thes seemed to have forgotten that Fenn was there. All expression had left his face. He sat totally still. Not even an eyeblink. The blood seemed to have drained out of him. He looked like a waxwork. But Fenn saw the faint rise of his chest; he was still breathing.

Fenn's own breathing slowed as he sat with his eyes on Thes, waiting for him to show he knew he was there.

Through the silence Fenn became aware of the humming. A high-pitched humming. He looked around, but with no hope that he'd see what was making the sound or where it was coming from. It wasn't unpleasant. In fact, it was sort of interesting, although it was all on the same note. He tried to copy it softly, under his breath, so as not to disturb Thes.

No, that wasn't quite it.

'Almost,' said Thes. 'Listen!'

He hit the note exactly, making it louder, then softer, then louder.

'Only the Keepers have the note,' he said.

Fenn paused, wondering how to phrase the question in a way that might get a satisfactory answer.

'Is the humming here, always?' he asked.

Thes nodded.

So the Yeti had nothing to do with it. That's one question answered, thought Fenn. It must be another extraordinary natural phenomenon.

Thes asked if he was comfortable, and gave a

whistling which suggested to Fenn that he was about to be asked something important.

'I shall make your Happening. It is my happiness to do so.' Thes gave a gracious smile. 'But it's not possible for you to take it with you. I must ask, either you keep it with you until you go, or leave it here with us.'

Fenn understood at once – Thes didn't want him to take away evidence of his time with the Yeti. This wasn't the occasion, he felt, to say that he wasn't planning to go, ever.

'Please, I'd like to leave it here with you, Sir.'

'Then, we begin,' said Thes. He reached into a grass-woven basket the young Keeper must have brought in with the goatskins. He took from it a handful of clay, and a thin sliver of flint, sharpened to a point. 'You tell me your Happening,' he said, 'one that you wish to remember. Then, I shall make it.'

Fenn had not given any thought to what his Happening might be. 'Before I came to live with the Yeti, nothing much happened to me, really.'

'Take your time, Fenn.'

'Nothing much happened…' he said again, and his voice trailed off.

The humming was zinging inside his head.

It was hot. He was starting to sweat.

His chest was tight. He couldn't breathe.

The room was whizzing around him.

Fenn closed his eyes.

He saw the tall grass.

The bush ablaze with flowers.

The suitcase gaping wide.

A yellow jumper, his dad's birthday jumper.

His mum's blue skirt.

Maybe Mum and Dad weren't already dead.

He should have got them out of the plane.

But he'd just lain there, by the bush, in the grass.

Waiting for the explosion.

Then, it was too late.

Fenn sprang to his feet.

'I don't want to be here!'

He looked wildly around him.

'I want to go home. I want Mum. I want Dad.'

His legs trembled under him.

He fell to his knees.

He was suddenly sobbing.

'I'll tell you my Happening!'

He looked up, directly at Thes, to make sure he understood. 'I'll tell you why I want you to make it.' His voice blazed with self-hating rage. 'I want you to make it so I'll know it's here for as long as I live. So I'll know that someone, for always, for ever, will know that I killed Mum and Dad.'

'Tell me how it happened,' said Thes, as if he was asking about an ordinary thing.

Afterwards, Fenn sat with his arms gripped round his knees, his eyes shut, the salt of his tears sharp on his lips. Thes came over beside him. They sat there for a long while.

13.

Fenn had stopped crying. He felt empty, as if he'd been washed inside. He didn't think he had any tears left.

He had told it all, about the plane, how he'd known it was unsafe, how he'd kept quiet about it. Things he'd forgotten came back. The change in the sound of the engine. Someone yelling, 'Get your head down!' The rush of air, the roaring of engines. The sodden ground, red with his blood. The song of the bird.

'I hate birds,' he burst out. 'I'll always hate birds. Birds have wings, like a plane.'

He could see that Thes was still struggling to grasp the idea of a bird-like thing that Humans flew in, but he accepted that it was so.

'If you say to your parents about the plane, what then?' he asked.

Fenn hadn't thought of that. He shrugged. 'They'd have thought I was being silly or I was scared or something.'

'What must you do, so they don't go in the plane?'

'I could have… well, I could have done something.'

Thes was waiting for him to go on. 'I could have…' Fenn's voice trailed off. 'Well I could have done something,' he repeated, aware that it wasn't much of an answer.

'You yourself are afraid, but still you go in the plane?'

'Well, I had this feeling about it, but it didn't make sense. It certainly wouldn't have made sense to Mum and Dad. They wouldn't have believed me. I didn't believe me… until it was too late.'

'And for this, you are saying that you kill your parents?'

'But I did! I could have saved them.'

'How?' Thes pressed gently. 'If they do not believe your Knowing?'

Fenn looked away. It was better to believe it was all his fault. It meant that things could have been different. It gave him the feeling they still could be different, and somehow Mum and Dad were coming back.

'But they're not. Are they?'

'No,' said Thes.

Fenn shut his eyes. The fact that Thes had spoken it

made it real, for the first time. His parents were dead. Since the crash it had seemed more like a dream than real. But it felt real now. It hurt, as if a sharp blade had pierced through him. But the hurt didn't make him want to cry any more. Or do anything.

'I'll never forget them,' he whispered.

'Of course not.' Thes put his hand on his heart. 'You loved them, and they loved you.'

'Yes. I know.'

'It is the Yeti way, for mother and father to wish happiness for their little ones. What is the Human way?'

Fenn's face lit up. 'The same. It's one thing that *is* the same.'

'It's not easy to be happy in a sorrow like yours. Not even for a Yeti. The Yeti way is –' Thes cupped his hands – 'to hold sorrow and happiness, both, together. The happiness warms the sorrow like the sun warms ice in the river, and at last the ice melts, and the river flows sweetly on.'

'Isa said something like that. She is going to be a Keeper, you know.' Fenn gave a hint of a smile. 'But of course you do!'

Thes talking about the river reminded him of the fish that he'd caught. He remembered he'd felt a little bit sad, but mostly proud, and when he'd arrived at the Keepers, he was certainly happy that he had something to give to Thes.

'That's what I would like for my Happening,' he burst out. 'Can you do that? Me, holding the fish. It was about this big.' He measured it out with his hands.

'Yes, I remember,' said Thes. He looked at Fenn closely. 'Are you sure, Fenn?'

'Yes, I am.' He had photographs and other keepsakes of his parents. 'Dad and Mum loved the Sanaskars, that's why we came. They always wanted to meet a Yeti themselves. I can tell you, they'd be thrilled about me being Yeti Boy!'

His face flushed happily at the thought of it. 'My Happening can be for them. Me, Yeti Boy, with my fish!' He knew he couldn't take it with him. 'Can I see it when you've made it?'

'Of course you can, Fenn. It shall be done at once.'

Thes took the ball of clay. He sprinkled it with a finely-ground powder, then flattened it to an oval shape with his hand. He placed it on the floor before him. He sat with that absolute stillness. Fenn held his breath, his eyes fixed on Thes. He felt as if Thes was beaming into his head. He watched, not moving himself, as Thes picked up the sharpened sliver of flint. He drew quickly, without lifting it once.

'There, it is done,' said Thes.

Eagerly Fenn bent forward to look.

'Wait!'

Thes rose and went towards a narrow slit in the wall. He placed the clay drawing into it, then sat down again. He gave a whistling. A few minutes later, four other Keepers came in and silently sat down too.

Now what? thought Fenn, certain that he was about to witness something extraordinary, though what, he couldn't imagine.

It began softly, the same note as the humming which he had heard earlier. It grew louder, softer, louder, then changed pitch to something that was neither a note nor a humming – an indescribable sound. Fenn had never heard one like it. It was making him tingle as if all the cells in his body were shot through with electric sparks. He felt warm and cool both at once. The sound flowed around and through him. It lifted him up, he was floating on it. He couldn't feel the ground beneath, just the air vibrating.

'Fenn.'

He heard his name coming from far away. He opened his eyes. He was still in the room, sitting on the floor. Thes was standing, but the other Keepers stayed seated.

Thes beckoned and Fenn went, a little unsteadily.

'Here is your Happening, Yeti Boy. Take it.'

Thes pointed to the slit in the wall. Fenn reached in. He could tell at first touch this wasn't clay he was holding. When he looked, he gasped aloud.

The grey clay had turned to a shimmering silver. Fenn saw himself engraved on it. He was holding the fish, as he had held it when he had offered it to Thes. In his face he saw the awe he had felt, and the pride in the fish. But also there was something else – in his eyes he saw deep sorrow. It was him, exactly, at that moment: it was just the way it had happened.

Fenn went over to where Thes was standing.

'Thank you,' he said, and bowed. He didn't feel ridiculous; it was what he wanted to do.

A girl Keeper, with white flowers braided into her hair, gestured him to follow her. The other Keepers went too, but not Thes. He had told them where to put Fenn's Happening, and they took him to a small circular room. It was the only room he'd seen with what looked, impossibly, like a glass ceiling. Whatever it was, he could see the sky through it.

There were five other engraved Happenings on the wall. Before Fenn could view them, he felt a tap on his shoulder.

'Thes says my Happening is to go here also.'

'Arkon!'

'I have had my Happening made too. Look!'

The craftsmanship wasn't quite as skilful as Thes's, but Fenn recognised himself at once, with Arkon, on the mountain, at the moment that they'd first seen each other. Their faces mirrored their looks of startled surprise.

Arkon pressed the engraving into the wall. It stuck at once.

'You and me, Yeti Boy.'

Fenn pressed his own engraving next to it.

'Yeti Boy catches fish!' he said.

The Keepers gathered to say goodbye. Fenn hoped to see Thes, but supposed he must be too busy. He realised what an honour it was to have been given so much of his time already, and that Thes had made his Happening.

'Before we go, there's something I must do!' he said suddenly.

They were standing outside the entrance into the

Keepers' mountain. Fenn paced about, testing the ground beneath. This was the place! He would plant Isa's peach stone here. He made a hollow for it, then took his water bottle from his backpack and watered it.

'Isa will be able to see the peach tree whenever she wants, when she comes to live here. It'll help her to remember me.'

'Isa will indeed remember you, Fenn,' said Thes, who had arrived unnoticed. He beckoned, and took Fenn aside.

'I wish you to take this with you,' he said. 'I was going to crush it to dust with a rock, but I'd rather no trace of it remained here, in our place.'

He handed Fenn something wrapped in woven grass, like a parcel. It was a small revolver, black and sleek. Fenn had never held a real gun before, but he could see at once it had three bullets left.

'Where was it found?' he asked. 'Is it the one that killed Ruala's brother?'

'It was found,' said Thes simply, and Fenn knew that was as much of an answer as he was going to get. He rewrapped the revolver, and put it in his backpack. He could understand why Thes wanted it removed, like litter, from the Yeti's land. But there was something he wanted to ask.

'It's not about the revolver—'

Thes smiled. 'You want to know how it is that we Keepers learn to make the Happenings with the whistling?'

'Yes. I've been wondering.'

'I will tell you what I was told. We learn from the Ones Who Came First.'

'The Ones Who Came First,' Fenn repeated. 'Who were they exactly?' As he voiced the question, he knew it would get no answer.

'That is all I can tell you,' said Thes. He placed his hands on Fenn's shoulders and gave a whistling that made him tingle all over. Then, he was gone.

'He really is something,' breathed Fenn.

Arkon came over to join him. The Keepers were going too. They went back into the mountain, with a bright, clear whistling. Fenn and Arkon could still hear it when they crossed the stream, to set off on their wander-about.

14.

After leaving the Keepers, Fenn and Arkon took it in turns to choose which way to go next. Fenn had been responsible for a few disasters. The latest had led them into a bog, and they'd spent the night being supper for hungry mosquitoes.

'Sorry, Arkon. But you told me to choose the direction my feet wanted to go!'

'You weren't listening to them properly! But always on a wander-about, it's sometimes good, and sometimes –' Arkon scratched at a bite – 'not good.'

The country was much as Fenn had seen it before, lightly wooded with open patches of grass and fruit trees and flowers. Now, they were in a forest where

112

trees grew densely. The birds made shrieks and harsh cries, and the buzzing, chirruping and humming of insects sounded as if they'd turned up the volume and were competing to be heard. The flowers were of brilliant colours – red, orange, yellow – some large as trumpets. Their scent was more sickly than sweet.

Fenn paused to watch the white-tailed monkeys that jumped from treetop to treetop overhead. The warm sunny valley where he lived with Arkon had come as a surprise. But this was like a jungle! To the outside world, the Sanaskars were bleak mountains with ice and snow. He knew what they were *really* like. Fenn smiled to himself as he ran to catch up with Arkon.

'Yeti Boy, stay close!' Arkon spoke calmly, but with unmistakable warning.

'What is it?' Fenn whispered.

Then he saw for himself. Arkon put a restraining hand on his shoulder. But Fenn could not have moved; he was frozen with terror.

An elephant that looked as big as a house moved out from the bamboo before them. It let out a thunderous roar and splayed its ears wide to display enormous yellowed tusks. Fenn watched as if he was seeing it on a screen in slow motion. The elephant was preparing to charge. It lifted a weighty foot. It pawed the ground. It was coming towards them.

From somewhere came a low, steady whistling. It went softer, then louder, then softer, till it stayed somewhere between. Through a gauze of fear, Fenn realised that it was Arkon.

The elephant snorted, flicked its trunk, turned and sauntered off. Soon, in the distance, they heard trumpetings as it rejoined its herd. Fenn sat down before his legs collapsed under him.

'I thought we'd had it. If you hadn't…' His voice trailed off.

'There wasn't big danger,' said Arkon. 'It just needed telling that we meant it no harm and the whistling gave warning to do no harm to us.'

Fenn looked anxiously over his shoulder. 'Does the whistling always work?'

'If it didn't, I'd be shaking with fear like you! Not even a Yeti has the strength to take on an elephant, or a tiger either. For all animals, the whistling is different.'

Fenn gulped. 'Tigers! Here?'

'Also, rhino. It's their place.'

'Great!' muttered Fenn. 'Rhinos, tigers and wild house-sized elephants!'

His heart leapt at the sound of something cracking underfoot. Then he realised it was a stick he had trodden on himself. He'd feel a bit safer if he could do the whistling like Arkon. Two of them doing it would be better than one.

'Will you teach me?'

Arkon shook his head. 'Whistling is no good if there is fear in it. But I learn you the Bee Sound. It sends the bees off from their nest. Then, up you go, and get honey! If you are stung it's not the end of you. But tigers—'

'No need to spell it out,' said Fenn quickly. 'Is there any animal the whistling doesn't work on? Just so I know.'

'The snow leopard. It lives by itself, always alone, and does as it wants. We have no whistling to calm it, or to warn it away.'

'They… um… don't hang around here, do they?'

'The snow leopard? You see snow? You think this is a snow place when the sun is so hot you sweat in it?'

It wasn't just the sticky heat that was making him sweat. It was the prospect of being savaged or eaten by a wild animal, thought Fenn. But Arkon's absence of fear reassured him. Soon they passed by a tigress watching over her cubs tumbling over each other. They were like kittens playing about in the garden. Fenn turned back to watch.

'This is a brilliant wander-about!' he said. 'When will you teach me the Bee Sound?'

'No time like the now!'

Arkon pointed to a bees' nest in a tree just beyond. He made a sound so highly pitched, Fenn could hardly hear it. But the bees swarmed out of the nest. Arkon skimmed the tree and scooped out a handful of honeycomb, oozing liquid gold.

'Easy as a catching a fish!' he said.

Fenn laughed. 'Yes, and I know how easy that is!'

They walked on and on. The forest gave way at last to grassland, which in turn gave way to tall growing pine trees. It was cooler here. A small river flowed swiftly over silvery stones. As if to keep pace with it,

Fenn and Arkon quickened their step.

The sight before them stilled them both.

Arkon gripped Fenn by the shoulder.

'It's the Forever Water. I have heard of it, and now, I see it!'

He raced down over the narrow stretch of sand and dipped his fingers in the water.

'It tastes salty – like skin – like they say! We stay here!' he said, beaming. 'My feet don't want any more wander-about.'

'Nor mine!' grinned Fenn. This is really something!' A saltwater lake so huge he couldn't see where it ended! Millions of years ago it must have been part of the sea. Maybe here he'd find a saligram at last.

There were no caves to sleep in, and although the nights were mild, they made a shelter of branches and grasses which they plaited together. The days merged into each other seamlessly. They swam and fished; they gathered roots, leaves, berries and birds' eggs; they chatted, made up whistling jokes and Fenn spent hours practising the Bee Sound.

But now, he was staring out at the sea.

The beach they had chanced upon was cut off by thick undergrowth at either end. He had tried swimming round as far he could. He was curious to see what was beyond.

'What we need is a boat, Arkon.'

At Arkon's puzzled look, Fenn drew a boat in the sand.

'It floats on the water,' he explained. They couldn't make a boat. But a raft! 'We could get some branches and bind them together with vines.'

'No vines here,' Arkon reminded him.

'Then we'll use something else.' Fenn's excitement was mounting. 'A raft can't be that hard to make. I bet we could do it.'

'For what?' Arkon was puzzled.

'So we can have a look round, for one thing.'

Arkon looked even more puzzled. 'It's good here.'

'I know. But…'

'But you want to float on the water, and not be here?'

'I didn't say that,' said Fenn. 'But I'm getting bored with fishing, swimming, eating, doing the same things.'

'Bored?' Arkon shook his head, baffled. 'What's that?'

'Well… it's just… Oh, forget it! But I'm going to have a try at making a raft.'

'You want to make your float-on, you make it!'

Arkon stretched out on his stomach, plucked a strand of grass, pulled it tight between his fingers, and blew it. It made a sweet high-pitched sound.

Abruptly he tossed it aside.

'It brings thinking to me of Ruala. She can make grass music the best.'

Something in Arkon's voice caught Fenn's attention.

'Was Ruala your girlfriend?' He put his hand on his heart to show what he meant. 'She was, wasn't she?'

Arkon didn't answer but he went a slight pink.

'It's because of me Ruala's gone off you. I should have realised before.' Fenn was furious with himself. 'I'm sorry, Arkon.'

'Don't get yourself in a bother, Yeti Boy. Before I save you, Ruala was "off me" as you say. After Joz, it is not only me Ruala is hating, it is all of us. I ask the Most Ancient if it will always be so. She said, if I wait, I will see.'

Arkon sighed, got up and went down to the sheltered end of the beach. For a while he just sat, gazing out over the lake. Then he turned to the sand-painting he'd begun that morning.

Small heaps of sand and earth were neatly set out according to the different colours and shades. He let his eyes run over them, then he reached for the one he would work with next. From amongst the pine trees, he heard Fenn crashing about.

When Fenn emerged, he was staggering under an armful of branches. 'Whew! They're heavy! And the needles are sticking into me.'

Arkon sat on his heels and laughed.

'Okay, I know you think I'm a diphead!' Fenn dumped down the wood. Having decided to have a go at making the raft, he'd give it his best shot. He picked up what he called his knife, a sharpened flint, and set to stripping the branches bare.

'Ouch!'

For the umpteenth time he cut himself as the flint slipped. How things got invented without proper tools he couldn't imagine. But at least he hoped to have something solid to show for all his effort – more than be could said of the sand-picture that Arkon was making. Like all the others, this latest would be blown away by the night breeze.

'I don't know how you can be bothered to start. It'll be gone almost as soon as you've finished.'

'I like to make sand-pictures, so I do. What's wrong with that?'

'Nothing's wrong with it. I just don't see the point of it.'

'That's because you're not a Yeti!' Arkon retorted, and turned his attention back to the painting with its mosaic-like pattern. From between his fingers he gently let fall grains of sand that had almost no colour by themselves, but together made a striking pink beside a bright yellow triangle. He couldn't resist calling Fenn to look.

'What do you say, Yeti Boy!'

'Wow, it's beautiful, Arkon.' It reminded Fenn of a stained-glass window – except that stained glass lasted for hundreds of years. Then he remembered that glass was made of sand. After he'd finished the raft, maybe he'd give it a try! Fenn smiled. There was lots here to keep him busy. He'd get on with the raft later. He was determined to finish it, but there was no hurry.

Fenn lay back.

Closed his eyes.

Listened to the *whssh* of the water as it edged ashore.

He felt – how did he feel?

Peaceful? Happy?

He groped for the words, but couldn't find them. He began to experiment with a whistling that would express how he was feeling just then.

He was startled by Arkon shaking his shoulder.

'We must go, Yeti Boy.'

'But you were just saying you wanted to stay. I was thinking how good it was here—'

'I am saying, now, we must go home!' cut in Arkon.

'What's brought this on?' muttered Fenn. Was it talking about Ruala? People acted weird when they were in love. But whatever it was, he wasn't going to argue. He'd never seen Arkon in such a state. He looked frantic.

'Of course we'll go, if you say,' he said. 'When do you want to leave?'

'This very now! At once!'

Arkon began to move off. He glanced back at the sand-painting, and went to brush it away with his foot. 'Let the wind have it,' he said, and turned and strode off.

'Wait, Arkon, I'm coming!'

Fenn looked back regretfully at the stacked branches that were to have been his raft. He'd never know now if he'd have got it to float.

They pressed on during every hour of daylight. Arkon scarcely spoke. If Fenn hadn't foraged food for them, he wouldn't have troubled to eat. As soon as they reached the Yeti valley he charged ahead, leaving Fenn to find his own way.

'Fenn, Yeti Boy!'

'Isa!'

Eagerly, Fenn ran to meet her. He slowed to a stop. Whatever had happened? Isa looked in shock, and very distressed.

'The Yellow Sickness has come,' she trembled. 'So many are dying already. It is the end of the Yeti!'

Isa covered her face, and wept.

15.

As the last of the daylight faded, Fenn and Arkon went to their cave and set about lighting a fire. They'd been so busy since they'd got back, it was the first occasion to rest. Together with the few who were well enough, they tended the sick, fetching water for them to drink and bathing their fevered foreheads.

The sickness began with a yellowing of the skin. This was followed by a fever. When it peaked – and the time for this varied – the end was quick to follow. Fenn was devastated to realise how many of the Yeti were stricken. Sturdy youngsters, like Isa, had escaped infection, but some of the elders had died already. Fenn asked the question he had not ventured to ask before.

'How is the Most Ancient?'

'She has the fever,' said Arkon.

Fenn threw a stick on to the fire and watched it catch light.

'Arkon, there *must* be a cure. You cured me, and I was as good as dead.'

'You had cuts and a common fever. The Yellow Sickness is different.' Arkon paused and stared into the fire. Without looking up, he went on, 'Till now, I think the Yellow Sickness is only a story.'

'A story?'

'All Yeti know it, about how, long before, near the beginning, it suddenly came. Yeti were dying fast as rain can fall. Then, a young Keeper who is called Shastiri wakes from a sleep one morning with a Knowing that leads her to Visigura Mountain. Yeti do not want to go there, because it is the place of the snow leopard, but Shastiri goes all the same. There, she finds plants she has never seen before. At once she picks them. She hurries back, and makes a mixture of them with water, to cure the sickness.'

'And did it?'

Arkon shrugged. 'That is the story. The Keepers have a Happening, of when she finds the plant.'

'That means it must be true,' said Fenn.

'No, Yeti Boy. Not true like you and me sitting here. There are all sorts of Happenings. A dream is a Happening. So is a story. The Keepers will make it for you to remember, if you want.'

What Arkon had told him about Shastiri reminded

Fenn of ancient myths where heroes, by miraculous feats, saved their people from death and disaster. But the Yellow Sickness wasn't a myth. It was happening right now.

'Arkon—'

There was no need for Fenn to go on.

'You and me have the same thinking, Yeti Boy. We'll leave for Visigura at sun-up.' Arkon looked him straight in eye. 'You do not have to come with me.'

'Oh yes I do,' said Fenn. There was a chance in a million they would find the plant, if it existed. Another chance in a million that it would cure the sickness. But he wasn't going to let Arkon go alone to Visigura.

Fenn woke with the first morning light. Arkon was already up. He set out the apricots and roots that he'd gathered.

'There is not much to eat on Visigura. It is not like here. It's too early for snow but there is always wind and cold. You must take your make-you-warm things.'

'How long will it take us to get there? Is it far?'

'Not so far. But hard walking. Burso tried to go. The fever came on him, and he had turn back.'

Fenn hunted out the clothes that had not been worn since he'd first arrived, and stuffed them into his backpack. Later, they could put the plants in it. He put on his boots, too. Then he collected up the left-overs from breakfast to take with them. It reminded him of the last time he'd stocked up with provisions – when he'd left the base camp for what he'd thought was a day's outing. It seemed forever ago.

The valley would normally be bustling at this time of morning with Yeti on their way to fetch water and food, pausing to chat and exchange whistlings. Now, even the birds and insects were silent. A solitary figure hurried by. He looked to see who it was.

Ruala!

She carried a tall water pot on her shoulder. If she had the sickness, thought Fenn, she wouldn't be up and about and moving so swiftly; but she looked thinner.

'Ruala is wearing herself away, looking after the sick ones,' said Arkon, who'd noticed her also. 'But still she can frown at me like thunder and glare like fierce sun. I tried to talk to her when we got back, but...' He brushed his hand across his forehead as if to get Ruala out of his mind.

'Arkon! Yeti Boy!'

It was Isa. They went quickly to meet her, but fearing the news she might bring. With relief they heard the Most Ancient was no worse and she wanted to see them.

'I'm looking after her,' said Isa.

'By yourself?' asked Fenn.

Isa drew herself up. 'I'm big enough. Come, the Most Ancient is waiting.'

Enough daylight filled the cave for Fenn to see the Most Ancient clearly. Her face was tinged with yellow and had shrunk into itself. Her body seemed to have shrunk too. But her eyes were clear and bright. Isa leant forward to sponge the beads of fever-sweat from her forehead but the Most Ancient waved her away, and turned to Arkon and Fenn.

'You are going to Visigura,' she said. 'Listen to what I tell you.'

The Most Ancient looked so small and frail that Fenn wondered how she had the strength to speak. But her voice was powerful, as if she was fuelled by an invisible fire inside.

'At Visigura, you must go to the peak where it is highest,' she said. 'The flower is white, with round petals. It has leaves that are like a star. You must bring both the leaves and the flower, as Shastiri did long before.'

'So, Shastiri isn't just a story!' said Fenn.

'Certainly, we Keepers believe Shastiri lived here, long before,' said the Most Ancient.

'All we Keepers believe it was so,' said Isa.

The Most Ancient stretched out her hands, one to Arkon, the other to Fenn. Her grip was strong.

'You take with you my thinking, and that of all Keepers, and all Yeti.'

She relaxed her grip, closed her eyes, and leant back.

The interview was over.

Isa went a little way down the path with them.

'I wanted to come with you to Visigura. But the Most Ancient says she cannot manage without me.'

'I'm sure that's true.' Fenn said. 'Remember the peach you gave me? I planted the stone for you. It's just outside where the Keepers live.'

'That is a good place, Yeti Boy!'

Fenn wanted to say something more to cheer her up.

'For my Happening, guess what Isa! It was me, holding the fish I caught myself.'

'You caught one! At last!'

But Isa's bright smile quickly went. 'The Sickness brings so much sorrow. I didn't know there could be such sorrow.' She attempted a smile. 'I'll try to be happy that you and Arkon are brave, like Shastiri – and that you go to Visigura to save the Yeti.'

'You're brave too, Keeper Isa,' said Fenn.

They hurried back to the cave where he had left his backpack. Arkon went to say a quick goodbye to Burso and Cheb, who were in the first stages of fever. It gave Fenn the opportunity he'd been hoping for. Checking that Arkon wasn't in sight, he made his way quickly to the river. As he hoped, he found Ruala there, returning yet again to fetch water for those who couldn't do so themselves.

At his footstep, she turned. Fenn knew what Arkon meant by her fierce and glaring look.

'Ruala, wait, please!' He gave a whistling that expressed the urgency of his plea better than words.

'What is it?' she rapped out.

'I know you hate me. I'd hate me if I was you. But Arkon is your true friend. He...' Fenn stumbled over the word; it felt a bit soppy but no other would do. 'Arkon loves you, you know.'

Ruala's mouth tightened. 'If he did, he would not

bring you here, after what you Humans did to my brother.'

'He didn't mean to. In fact, if Arkon had his chance again, I don't think he would. It just happened and you know, with a Happening, there's nothing you can do about it. Like you couldn't stop what happened to Joz. Like I couldn't help what happened to my mother and father, though I felt that I killed them.'

'Killed your mother and father!' Ruala's eyes widened with horror.

'I felt it should be me who was dead,' said Fenn. 'That it was wrong to be alive. You know what I mean?'

Ruala didn't answer, but he saw she understood all too well.

'I hated everyone and I wanted everyone to hate me because I deserved it.' Fenn heard, as from a distance, the tears and rage in his voice. It was as if he had turned back into who he was then.

'I wanted everyone to hate me as much as *I* hated me,' he said. 'But the trouble was, nobody could. No one could hate me that much.'

Ruala gave a moan, and hid her face in her hands. Her shoulders shook, tears ran through her fingers. Fenn moved to go towards her, but no, she wouldn't want him near, and he had only a few moments before Arkon would come looking for him.

'Ruala, don't let Arkon go away with you hating him. Make it up with him.' He didn't say it, but it was plain enough that with the sickness threatening and

128

the dangers of Visigura, she mightn't have the chance again.

I've blown it, I haven't got through to her, he thought, as without a word, Ruala turned and fled.

He got back to the cave just before Arkon, and humped his backpack onto his shoulders.

'You take the mountain with you, Yeti Boy!'

'That's how it feels! It's got all my clothes in it. I'll put them on later. Let's go.'

They set off towards the north of the valley. Some of the Yeti, pale and sick with fever, came to the entrance of their caves to see them go. As they left the last dwellings behind them, they heard a whistling from above. It was Ruala. She stood on a rock that looked down on the track.

'Arkon!'

She gave a quick wave and a smile, that was all – but from Arkon's expression…!

'You've got it bad, ' grinned Fenn.

A bird began to sing in an tree nearby. Arkon's face lit up.

'It's a good sign, Yeti Boy.'

'Yes, we can hope so,' said Fenn.

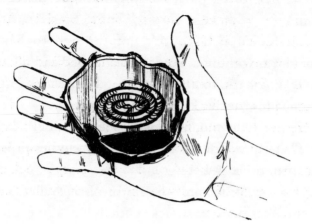

16.

Fenn shivered as he zipped up his anorak. For the first time since he'd come to live with the Yeti, he felt cold.

The Sanaskars were like a miniature version of the Himalayas with the range of terrain and climate. It was amazing how suddenly the weather had shifted, no longer warm and sunny as it was in the valley. The chilled landscape was ruggedly bleak and the wind was bone-freezing here. At last, reluctantly, he'd put on his warm clothes. After the freedom of bare arms and legs, long sleeves and trousers felt stifling. So far Fenn had resisted the thermals, but he would need them soon. As he looked up, he could see how the few straggling trees thinned out to rock and wind-torn grass. It was lucky the winter hadn't moved in just yet. He'd never have been able to make it through snow. So deep, Arkon said, it came over his head.

They made their way in silence, saving all their strength for the task before them. Occasionally they exchanged whistlings, less tiring than talking.

Despite the wind, Fenn was sweating as he struggled up to the broad ledge where Arkon was waiting. Arkon stretched a hand to help him up. A craggy rock shelf hung above them, giving shelter. A clump of bushes took shelter there too.

'Honeysuckle! I don't believe it!'

Fenn picked one of the slim, trumpet-shaped flowers, nipped off the green cup at the base, and sucked. Not exactly bee honey, but not bad! They had eaten most of their provisions, and now they were surviving on small, deep-purple berries that were hard and rather bitter, and some kind of creepy-crawly that Arkon found. It had been too windy for a fire, so Fenn would shut his eyes, think of something like pizza or chips, and swallow the creepy-crawly, raw.

He looked enviously at the goats that bounded lightly past, while he had to struggle for each step. He watched till they scampered out of sight, then flexed his shoulders, ready for the next climbing stint.

'It will be sundown soon,' said Arkon. 'It's best we stay here.'

Fenn was only too glad to agree. They pulled away the honeysuckle from the rock, to make a den behind it.

Arkon sat staring into the distance. Now they

weren't on the move, his anxieties about those at home crept over him. The Arkon who boldly led the way was lost in despairing grief, as if he had become someone else. Fenn knew how he was feeling. But he couldn't offer comforting words. He couldn't say, 'It will be all right.' Things were not always all right, and others pretending they would be made it worse.

He eased himself against his backpack which served as a pillow. He could tell by his trousers that he'd grown taller. The muscles in his arms and legs were firmer than they used to be, but he was still quite skinny. With the Yeti, Fenn spent much of his time gathering food, but when you added it up he thought, he didn't actually eat a lot. Now, he would have to get by on a few berries and grubs.

To take his mind off his stomach, Fenn began to scratch at the earth with a stick. He knew exactly what he was looking for.

The gravel soon gave way to fine sand. He uncovered a scattering of stones, all of them grey. He sent them hurtling down the slope. Then, by his foot, he saw two black stones. Quickly he hunted for something to crack them open with. This should do it! He gripped a small rock that fitted snugly into his hand. He began to hammer at the larger of the black stones, beating out a rhythm. It caught Arkon's attention, and he began to clap in time with it.

Fenn speeded up the hammering.

'There could be a saligram inside this stone, Arkon.' He explained what it was – the imprint of a creature

that once swam in the sea.

'The sea? What is sea?' Arkon queried.

'Like Forever Water, only bigger,' said Fenn. 'If we find a saligram, we'll be finding a creature from long, long before. From the time before Humans, and Yeti too!'

Arkon looked at him in disbelief. But he was infected by Fenn's excitement and began to hammer at the other black stone.

'Go carefully when it starts to crack, Arkon. If it's got a saligram inside, you don't want to smash it.'

Fenn's hammering paid off at last. The stone split down the centre and he eased it apart.

'Arkon! Look! Just take a look!'

He held out the half of the stone that revealed the spiral shape of a tiny sea-creature.

'I have a little creature too,' said Arkon, displaying an identical spiral form in the broken black stone that lay in his huge palm.

'Wow!' breathed Fenn. His eyes were shining and his face lit with happiness and the glow of the setting sun. 'My dad said he'd dreamed of finding one of these ever since he was the same age as me.'

Fenn glanced down at the saligram.

'My dad's dead,' he said. 'My mum's dead too.' His voice wavered, but at least he could speak of his mother and father without his heart breaking apart, as the stone that held the saligram had done.

'I am thinking I know it already, about your mum and dad. I am sorry for that, Yeti Boy,' said Arkon. He brushed away the last of the sand, and offered the saligram to Fenn.

'Take my Finding. You have it,' he said.

Fenn went to protest, but he took it.

'You have the one I found. Fair's fair!'

They grinned at each other, hugely pleased by the exchange, and set up a whistling that had them breaking off into fits of laughter.

'I do not think Visigura has ever heard so much laughing,' said Arkon. 'But now we must sleep, Yeti Boy.'

Fenn knew something was amiss as soon as he opened his eyes next morning.

Arkon was awake, but he sat, shoulders hunched, and he was shivering. Seeing Fenn looking at him, he tried to control it, and said brightly, 'Maybe we get to the top this small sunaround.' He went to stand up but his legs gave way and he had to support himself on the rock. 'I'm getting old,' he joked.

No, please, no, Fenn silently pleaded. He'd count to three and when he looked again, Arkon's face would be its usual light tan. But it wasn't. There was no mistaking the yellow tinge of his skin and the yellowing whites of his eyes.

'We go, Yeti Boy.' Arkon took an unsteady step forward. 'We find food. You hungry? But of course, you're always hungry! Come!' He told Fenn to follow him exactly. 'Don't look down. Look at the place where you put your feet. That is the Yeti way, safe and slow.'

Fenn stayed where he was, but his mind was racing. Arkon had the Yellow Sickness. He already showed the first signs of the fever; sweat ran down his forehead and gleamed round his neck. He would drive himself on till he dropped. Drop as in drop dead, thought Fenn.

Fenn's legs were trembling, but not from fever. He was scared for Arkon. He slowed his breath and tried to calm his panicky feelings. He must think, think fast and think clearly.

Arkon had managed to heave himself a metre up the incline ahead. He was panting heavily. He wouldn't be able to go on for much further. It was best he stop now, thought Fenn. Here at least, there was shelter. Water, too — the stream they'd drunk from the night before was nearby.

'Arkon, I have something to say.'

'No time for talk.' Arkon turned his back, and went to move on. Fenn saw the effort it cost him.

'Arkon, you must stay here.'

'No!' The word exploded into the air.

'But you can't go on. You know you can't. Ask your Knowing.'

Arkon gave a sigh that brought tears flooding up inside Fenn, but he made himself swallow them down.

'It's true, isn't it?' he pressed gently.

'Yes.'

Now it was spoken, Arkon crumpled and sank to his knees and wrapped his arms around himself. He hid his face. 'The Sickness will take us all. There will be no more Yeti. For the Yeti, the time is over.'

'Not if I can help it,' said Fenn. 'I'm going on.' He gave a whistling that left no space for argument. 'You said we might make it to the top tonight. It might take me longer on my own, but not much. First, I'll get you some water.' He rummaged in his backpack. His hand hit the water bottle and something else. The revolver. He'd forgotten about it. He shoved it away, and hurried off to fetch the water.

When he returned – in that short time – Arkon had grown noticeably weaker. Fenn helped him into the deepest recess of the shelter. He was tempted to leave his anorak for Arkon to use as a blanket, but he knew that he would need it himself.

'Arkon, I'm going now.'

'Remember what I have told you,' urged Arkon. 'Watch your feet. Follow your Knowing. Don't get in a fluster. Be a good Yeti.'

'Yes, I will,' said Fenn.

'I am happy you happened, Yeti Boy. You are my best Happening!' Arkon beamed a smile, for a moment his old self. Then the fever shook him.

'Go!' he whispered. 'Go quick. Find the star plant for the Yeti.' His breath came in painful rasps, and he closed his eyes.

Fenn knelt closer beside him. 'Arkon, don't you die, you hear me! Just hold on till I get back. I *will* get back, you'll see!' Fenn was shaking as he held Arkon's hand, very tightly, in both his own. But he was no help to Arkon here.

He picked up his backpack.

He must find the star plant.

Fenn's face was determined as he set off for the peak of Visigura.

17.

'How much further is it, Hubbert?' asked Kate.

'Not far now. We're making good time.'

'I hope the porters are waiting for us, with the mules,' said Kate. 'It would be too bad to be let down for a second time.'

The scientists had arranged for a final delivery of supplies to see them through till they left the Sanaskars. The local man who'd promised to oversee it had let them down. Jack Hubbert had offered to take over and his offer had been gratefully accepted.

'But I'll need one of you to help me,' said Hubbert. He knew Kate was the obvious choice since she was ahead with her work. Reluctantly, Kate had agreed to go with him.

Now they were on the return journey, with the supplies loaded into the back of the jeep Hubbert had hired. Parts of the engine were held in place by string, but the owner had promised it wouldn't break down – unless a demon spirit put a curse on it!

'That's one misfortune we've been spared – so far!' muttered Hubbert, as the jeep jolted and groaned. He glanced at Kate.

'You know what I miss most on expeditions?' he said as he manoeuvred the jeep round a pothole. 'Fresh fruit and vegetables. After tinned and dried food, an apple is a treat, or even the humble turnip.'

'Never mind the turnips,' wailed Kate. 'I forgot to buy the chocolate!'

Hubbert pointed to the package behind her head.

'Chocolate!'

'You remembered it!' She almost smiled. 'If I'd got back without it, the others would never have forgiven me.'

'For you, anything, anytime, Katie Kildaire... And look!'

Not far ahead, a group of men were sitting on a stone wall, their mules grazing nearby. They were waiting, as arranged, to help take the supplies up the mountain to the camp.

This was as far as the road went. As Hubbert pulled the jeep to a grateful stop, the men strolled over. Hubbert gave instructions for loading the supplies onto the mules, then turned to Kate.

'Come on, Kate. It's best we leave them to it. There's an inn where we can get a cup of tea, and maybe biscuits too. It's rough and ready, but at least it'll be warm.'

They walked on into the small village that hugged the foothills of the mountain. The cobbled main street merged into a dirt track, worn deep over years. They stood aside to let a caravan of yaks pass by, packed high with bright woven fabrics.

'It all looks so bright,' said Kate. The houses were whitewashed and the temple painted orange, with a gold spire.

'Splendid isn't it? It's real gold leaf,' Hubbert told her. 'Even the poorest can enjoy the sight of it. I like that. Typical of Asharn. So is the inn,' he added.

The inn, as he'd warned, was rough and ready. The ground floor was used to stable the livestock that travellers brought with them – mules, horses, a few yaks, and numerous goats and sheep. They climbed a ladder to the floor above, which was crowded with men, woman and children. Some were asleep, stretched out on the floor, surrounded by bundles of all shapes and sizes. A fire was burning but there was no chimney, and the room reeked of smoke, human sweat and livestock.

'Jack Hubbert!' went up a shout, and a small man, with a gold front tooth, came up and hugged him. He was the owner of the inn. When he saw Kate, he quickly drew back. His look told her he knew who she was, and that he knew about Fenn. In fact, everyone seemed to know. Kate found herself the focus of unspoken sympathy as she sat on the cushion that Hubbert's friend had set out on the wooden floor. It had been just the same when they were in the village where they had bought the food.

'It makes me feel… I can't explain, but I don't like it, Hubbert. Let's go.'

'Have your tea, Kate.' He put his hand on her arm. 'Everyone knows about Fenn, not just here, but all over the Sanaskars, all over Asharn. It's the best chance that if he is found, we will get to hear of it.'

'But Fenn won't be found.' Kate had realised for some weeks that Hubbert no longer thought so. 'I'm right, aren't I?'

'I think it's unlikely now,' he said carefully.

'All this time, you've been having me on, Hubbert, letting me hope.'

'You don't really believe that,' he said, matter-of-factly. 'It's the first time a strong hunch has let me down. I was wrong. I'm sorry, Kate. I can't imagine regretting anything more.'

Kate shrugged, and turned away. She'd arrived at the Sanaskars believing it was going to be a specially happy time, not just for herself, but for James, Alice and Fenn, too. How differently things had worked out.

She sipped her tea; it tasted of woodsmoke. People were talking; a baby was yelling, despite his mother's soothing. A youth began to thump a small hand-drum. Kate shuddered. She wished she hadn't let Hubbert persuade her to leave the peace of the mountain.

Hubbert wished he could tell Kate he knew how much it was hurting. But it would hurt more when the scientists finally left the camp. Then it would hit Kate that all hope was gone and the search for Fenn was over. By taking Kate away for a few days now, Hubbert hoped it would be less brutal for her later.

'Do you want more tea? I can send for some.'

Kate shook her head. What a fool she'd been, to have taken hope from Hubbert's twaddle about the Yeti. As if an imaginary creature could have rescued Fenn.

'You were having me on about that footprint, Hubbert. You can't seriously believe it was made by a Yeti.'

'I do, actually.' He had taken photographs and made a plaster cast of it.

'Hardly evidence,' scathed Kate. 'Not what *I'd* call evidence. But then, you're not a scientist.'

'Oh? So what am I, Kate Kildaire?'

She blushed, realising he knew what she was thinking: that he was an adventuring roughneck.

'Which is true,' Hubbert laughed. 'Though, as it happens, I do have a day job. I come here, when I can, for vacations and sabbaticals, like now. I work for an institution that has the good sense to give me six months' leave every few years to replenish my brain cells, such as they are.'

'What work do you do?' Kate asked, making an effort not to show her surprise at what he had revealed.

'It'd take longer than we have now to go into it, but basically, I'm involved in stargazing.'

'Are you trying to tell me you're an astronomer?'

'Couldn't have put it better myself! I was about twelve when I got interested in astronomy. What grabbed me was the notion that up there, somewhere, was the key to how it all began, the Earth, the universe. At that age, I thought I'd find out any minute.' He laughed. 'But I'm still looking. The same as you, Kate.'

She glared back at him. But it was a coincidence, she thought, that she, Fenn's father and Hubbert too, had developed interests at about the same age – interests that would determine their futures. Twelve years of age – Fenn's age. But Fenn was dead, and his father too.

Her desire to squash Hubbert was trivial, Kate knew that. But it made her feel better, and she couldn't resist it. 'If you met another talking Yeti, what would you say to it?'

He took the question seriously. 'You know, I've never considered what I'd do if it actually came to it. But I *did* see one, Kate.'

'You'll find people in this room who'll swear they've seen demons too. They say they're on the mountain passes, and demand tributes of rice or whatever to let them go by safely.'

Hubbert smiled. 'I admit, I haven't seen any demons myself. But I don't claim that proves they're not there.'

Kate had no answer to that.

★

Back outside, the sun was bright, but it barely warmed the chill air – the summer was over. Kate zipped up her anorak and put up the hood. To her relief, the men had finished loading the supplies onto the mules and they could leave at once for the camp.

A few hours later, they reached the first of the mountain passes to be crossed. The wooden bridge swung unnervingly in the wind.

'We'll take a rest before we go on,' said Hubbert.

Kate walked off, alone, to shelter against a clump of rocks huddled close together as if seeking solace in this desolate place. She was tired, and very cold. The higher peaks were covered in snow. Soon, snow would cover the camp, she thought, and all trace of it would be gone. But Fenn would be here. His parents would be with him. All three would be together. Kate tried to find comfort in that.

'It's time to move on,' Kate heard Hubbert say. She saw the Head Porter put a handful of rice on a rock by the bridge. She asked him to give her some.

'It will bring you luck, Missy.'

'It's not for me,' she said.

Kate placed the rice carefully on the rock. The wind swept it up like a mighty breath, and she watched as her offering was carried away.

18.

The peak of Visigura was covered in cloud. It was difficult for Fenn to gauge his progress. He couldn't go directly upwards, only where he could find a way, which meant he was endlessly zigzagging back and forth. He had lost track of time and had no idea how many hours had passed since he'd left Arkon. His muscles ached as if they'd been battered, bruised and set on fire. But he focused on where he was going, and ignored the pain. He was getting tired, and this wasn't the place to let his concentration go.

He was standing on a narrow rock shelf with a crevice below. The shelf was on a spur that jutted up like a giant granite needle. Fenn didn't know if the shelf continued or stopped where he stood. He couldn't see round. He stretched out his leg. It hovered in mid-air. Desperately, he groped for a foothold. He didn't look down, but he knew there was a sheer drop below. He could feel it, like a cruel presence, trying to drag him down into it.

'You're not getting me, so shove off!'

It was crazy thing to say to an empty space. But he felt better saying it, while he considered what to do next.

If he couldn't find a way forward around the spur, he'd have to turn back and look for another route. That would mean extra time and he didn't have any to spare. He pressed himself more firmly into the rock-face and reached again for a foothold. This time he found one, and he began to edge his way round.

A tuft of coarse grass offered a handhold. Thankfully, he reached out and grabbed it. It came away, bringing with it a spattering of earth and stones. Fenn struggled to regain his balance. The stones fell, hitting his head, as they hurtled down. He nearly followed them. But just in time he remembered to test the grass that invitingly offered itself before he gave it his full weight. It was a close thing. He wiped away the fear-sweat that ran down his forehead. Then he looked to see where he was, and what lay ahead.

'I don't believe it! I do not believe it!'

He could see the peak of Visigura clearly now. The route up was a gradual slope littered with huge rocks and boulders. Could he make it before the light went?

He was desperate to find the star plant. He felt a surge of energy.

Off the spur at last, he began to push on, towards the peak.

'No! No,' he repeated, and came to a stop.

He knew plainly, as if he'd seen a neon sign, he must go no further. He was too tired. It wasn't safe to push himself on. He probably wouldn't make it to the top before the light faded, in any case. He'd certainly be too exhausted for the climb down. He'd have to be patient, and wait till tomorrow to know if the star plant grew on the peak. Now the decision was made he felt relieved, and he looked about for somewhere to spend the night.

He found a small cave deep enough to be dry. Goat droppings littered the floor. Fenn kicked them out and went to search for any bushes he could use for cover. Once the sun went down, the temperature would plummet. He wished he could light a fire, but even in a windless place he'd never even managed to get a spark from the friction of rubbing stones or sticks together. He'd better put on his thermals. It meant he'd have to take his clothes off first to put them on, but he'd make the effort. He was very hungry, but was too tired to look about for something to eat. He'd just have to stay hungry.

A violet flush swept over the sky as the deep blue of the day merged with the red of the setting sun. Fenn thought of Arkon, sick with the fever, and the tears started to come. I'll send him a whistling, he thought, maybe he'll hear it. He waited in the hope of a reply, but none came. At last, weariness overcame him and he drifted into an uneasy sleep.

During the night Fenn woke time and again from the cold. When morning broke he was eager to move on, but he had to wait till the sun dried off the night moisture from the rocks. It made them treacherously slippery, and he mustn't risk it.

As he waited, he saw an underground stream easing its way down a tumble of rocks. He cupped his hands to drink and caught his breath – it was like drinking liquid ice. He looked round for the purple berries to eat. His face lit up as if he'd found a roast dinner, ready and waiting, when he found a bush covered with them. He ate some, saving the others for later. He put them in an empty crisp packet he'd found in his anorak pocket, and tucked them into his backpack. Now, at last, it was safe to move on.

The way up wasn't as direct as it had looked from lower down. The easiest route wound up in a spiral. It was all taking much longer than he'd thought. His foothold slipped and the gravel slid away beneath him. He wasn't in danger of a serious fall, but it startled him. He was beginning to lose it. He must take a breather, just for a few minutes. He flung down his backpack and searched for the berries he'd saved. They were a bit squashed but better than nothing. He'd sit down to eat them. That rock would do. The top at least was flat.

Fenn clambered up, and on the ground, on the other side of the rock, he saw the goat. Or what was left of it. Its head was torn off, and lumps of flesh had been ripped off its carcass. It had been savaged to death, and he didn't need a hundred guesses to tell who'd done it. Arkon had told him that the snow leopard didn't gobble its prey all at once, but would eat some and return later for what was left.

Where was the snow leopard now? Not far from its next meal, he thought, glancing at the unfortunate goat.

Fenn took the revolver from his backpack, and put it in his anorak pocket. He had a good eye, so he should be able to shoot straight. But the sound of the revolver being fired should be enough to scare off the snow leopard. Then he remembered the goat. Fenn couldn't imagine the snow leopard being scared of anything. He told himself he was very unlikely to come across it. He would keep on the alert, but now he must push on to the peak.

It must be midday by now, he thought, glancing up at the sun. He had been climbing at a good, steady speed. He was almost there.

From the distance, the peak of Visigura looked like a spire, but as he got nearer, he saw it was flat, more like a platform than a peak. He wasn't complaining! He had one thought now, the star plant.

Let it be there, he willed it to be there.

If it wasn't…

He stopped.

He peered down.

Growing close to the ground, he saw a small white

flower with round petals and dark green leaves, unmistakably shaped like a star. This was the plant the Most Ancient had described. Fenn touched it lightly, brushing his fingers over it.

'You're going to save the Yeti!' he said. But he would need more than one plant. He scrambled on up. Now there was only the sky above him.

'I've done it! I've made it to the top of Visigura!'

The ground was covered with star plants.

Fenn gave an exultant shout. 'Yes, oh yes!'

On his hands and knees he pulled up both the flowers and the leaves, as the Most Ancient had told him. He filled his backpack and every pocket. He could carry no more.

Fenn stood up and stretched his legs, and looked around him.

The wind had eased. It was warm, pleasantly warm. The sky had cleared to a blue more brilliant than any he'd seen before, and brighter, as if it had been polished. The surrounding mountains rose higher than Visigura. Their peaks were covered with iced-over snow. The rays of the sun struck them and bounced off with a scattering of sparkling pinks and golds. In all this vastness, Fenn was just a little thing, a speck. It wasn't a cosy feeling, he thought. But it was brilliantly thrilling. He was here, alone. This was his place, all of it! The snow, the ice, the sun, the sky! He breathed deeply, inhaling it all inside him, so it would be part of him always.

'Now, I must go,' he said to himself.

The way up had been difficult. The way down was no easier, and it was more frightening. He had to look down for every foothold, and he could see what lay below if he slipped. He was beginning to tire again. Stop for a rest. He looked about for somewhere to sit.

Then he felt the eyes on him, from a high rock just ahead.

Fenn knew what it was.

His hand slipped into his pocket, and around the revolver.

The snow leopard stared down, with eyes like frosted glass. Black rosettes studded its fur, which was thick and grey. Its body tapered from powerful shoulders to muscled haunches. Its thick long tail, lashed back and forth. Otherwise, it was completely still.

Fenn, too, was still. His mind was clear as if fear had wiped it clean. He felt frozen inside, and not afraid. The snow leopard stood between him and Arkon and the way back to the Yeti. He had three bullets. He raised the revolver.

The snow leopard sprang. It landed on a ledge above him. Fenn swung round. He fell as he lost his balance. He lay on the ground, under the snow leopard's gaze. It flexed its shoulders. It launched itself high, slow and easy, as if Fenn wasn't worth the hurry. It rose in the air, up and over him. Then it was gone, and out of sight.

The fear that had kept itself at bay overwhelmed Fenn now. He lay trembling, unaware of the thorny bush that straggled over the ground and pierced his cheek. He would have killed the snow leopard – or tried to.

What else could he have done? But the snow leopard had spared him. He was lucky to be alive. He was lucky not to have suffered the same grisly fate as the goat.

Fenn put the revolver in his backpack. He could still feel its imprint, and he wiped his hand on the grass. He realised there was no way he could have scared – let alone killed – the snow leopard.

The snow leopard was a truly magnificent, mighty creature. This was its place.

It was *my* place, just for a moment, thought Fenn – a moment he'd always remember.

Fenn went slowly now. He was careful to avoid going near the goat carcass, but he didn't feel that he would see the snow leopard again. He was still shaken by the encounter. He mustn't let himself think of it. He mustn't think about Arkon or what might be happening to the Yeti at home. He must keep himself together, and think only where to put his feet.

He looked about for a foothold that would take his weight.

'Slow and steady,' said Fenn to himself.

19.

Fenn had almost reached the place where he had left Arkon. He paused, trying to calm himself, but his heart was stampeding wildly. His Knowing – good luck too – had got him to the peak of Visigura and back. But it didn't tell him how Arkon was, and that was all that mattered to him now.

'Arkon!' he called.

No answer.

He slid down the last of the slope. There was the honeysuckle bush.

'Arkon,' he whispered.

Arkon was lying, huddled up, with an arm flung loosely out. Fenn knelt down beside him. His forehead was so hot! But he was breathing.

'It's me, Yeti Boy. Can you hear me? I've got the star plant! It's going to make you better. You and all the Yeti.'

Arkon opened his eyes. He blinked and looked again.

'No, I'm not a dream. I'm really here,' said Fenn.

'That is good,' Arkon murmured.

'I'm going to get some water, and mix the plant with it, like the Most Ancient said. I won't be long.'

Fenn took the water bottle, and raced to the stream. He placed a handful of plants on a stone and mashed them to pulp. How many should he use? How much water should he add? He'd have to guess.

During the night, at intervals, he gave Arkon sips of the star-plant mixture. There was a full moon. He was glad of it keeping him company, watching over Arkon. But he couldn't keep his eyes open all night, and soon he fell into a deep sleep.

He woke the next morning to find Arkon sitting up.

'The fever is dropping away. The star plant is a good eater, Yeti Boy!'

Arkon tried to stand up.

'Don't you dare even think of it.' Fenn regarded him sternly. 'You're staying put.'

'Have no worry for me, Yeti Boy. You must go to the others.'

Fenn shook his head. 'I'm not leaving you, Arkon.'

Arkon gave an insistent whistling.

'All right, you win,' Fenn sighed. 'Just for a change,' he added, with the trace of a grin.

He made up more of the star-plant mixture. 'I'll leave you some more plants, too. But I think I should stay, just a little while. You need looking after, you know you do.'

Their eyes met.

'Stubborn! Just as I thought when I first met him,' muttered Fenn.

Fenn was upset at leaving Arkon, and it was some time before he realised that he had no idea how to get to the valley once he was off the mountain. It wasn't like getting to the peak of Visigura, when he knew the direction was upwards. But he couldn't mess things up now.

'Come on, Yeti Boy,' he urged himself. 'The sun, you diphead! Go by the sun.'

The valley was to the south, he knew that much. He glanced down at his feet.

'South, keep to the south, got it? This isn't a wander-about. You can't go taking me wherever you fancy. We need to get home, and fast.'

The backpack was cutting into his shoulders. He shifted it, trying to find a place where the straps hadn't already edged into his flesh. Some hope, he thought. He flexed his legs, trying to will more strength into them. He was walking like a robot. His mind was a blur. Gaps of time vanished. He'd suddenly find himself in a place with no memory of how he had got there.

Where was he now? Was he back in the Yeti valley at last, or was this another like it? That twist in the river, had he and Arkon swum there once? That tree, with the hollow trunk, was that where they'd found a prize hoard to make grub kebabs, or was it one like it? He thought he heard a whistling. He whizzed round. No one there.

I'm hallucinating.

Panic lurched him to a standstill. It hadn't occurred to him before that *he* might get the Yellow Sickness. He was immensely hot, his clothes were sweated through and he felt so weak he could scarcely stand. Was he hearing things, in the delirium of a fever?

Then, through the trees, he saw Ruala. She looked as he felt, like a ghost of herself, but she was real. He saw the fear in her face. Quickly he told her that Arkon was alive, and recovering.

'I found the star plant, and it works. It's not just a story, about Shastiri. I hope I'm not too late—'

'For some,' said Ruala.

Apart from a few of the little ones, Isa amongst them, she alone had escaped the sickness, and the care of the others had fallen on her.

'I can help now,' said Fenn. 'I'll be fine, once I've had a breather and something to eat.'

'I roast roots for you, Yeti Boy. Then, we make the star-plant mixture, the way the Most Ancient says. She is still with us.' Ruala gave a small smile. 'She tells us it is not the time for her to die. But I do not believe it, till now.'

Together with the children who'd escaped the sickness, they gave doses of the star plant as it was needed. At first, they made up the mixture one bowl at a time. But to save time and energy, they needed a system. Fenn suggested the present arrangement where he pounded the plants, Ruala scooped the mixture into the row of waiting bowls, and he topped them up with water.

She sat back on her heels, and pushed the hair from her face. 'I hope Arkon will not try to come back till he's properly strong,' she said. 'You say he has shelter where you left him?'

Fenn had lost count of how many times he'd told her just that! 'I know you're itching to go and see him.' But now everyone was on the mend, they needed food, which had to be fetched and prepared. They could just about manage between them. 'Besides, you're in no state for a long trek, Ruala. You'll have to wait a bit longer before—'

Fenn gave a whistling of what he thought was a brilliant description of gooey lovers.

'You get on with those leaves,' she said, turning away, but not before he'd seen her turn a very bright pink.

Cheb and Burso had already gone to take the star plant to Yeti beyond their valley who might have been stricken by the Yellow Sickness, and to tell them where to find more. Meanwhile, Fenn was overwhelmed with thanks, which was really embarrassing. He announced he'd had enough thanks to last for the rest of his life, and please, not to give him any more.

Then, one evening, he heard a whistling.

Arkon!

He ran to meet him. There he was!

They beamed at each other.

Arkon thumped his chest. 'I am bigger and stronger than ever, Yeti Boy!'

They whooped about crazily, and soon everyone knew that Arkon was safely home. His return marked the end of the crisis.

Fenn had been worried, secretly, that now Arkon had made it up with Ruala, he'd be left out. But the only difference was, instead of giving them dagger looks or the big freeze when she saw them, Ruala smiled as if sugar wouldn't melt in her mouth. At night, as they sat about the fire, Cheb, Burso and others came to join them, sometimes Ruala amongst them. But she never hung around for long. Then, Fenn realised why. She would have plenty of time to spend with Arkon, later.

The thought that Fenn had pushed away suddenly surfaced. He hadn't looked to check, but he was sure the sun must be nearing the White Bark Tree.

He was down by the water hole, doing his Tarzan act, when Isa came looking for him.

'The Most Ancient sent me to find you,' she said.

Fenn knew exactly why.

The Most Ancient beckoned Fenn to sit beside her. She looked frailer after the sickness, but her movements were steady, and her voice was as strong as before.

'When Arkon brought you to us,' she said, 'I knew that you should stay, but not for why. Now I know that also. You came as a gift to us, our Yeti Boy.'

'No, no,' he protested.

The Most Ancient smiled. 'Shall we say, you and the Yeti are a gift to each other?'

'But I have to go, don't I?'

Fenn saw the answer in her look. He couldn't ask to stay. It would seem as if he was seeking something in return for finding the star plant, and he just couldn't do it.

'This many small sunarounds will pass.' The Most Ancient held up three fingers. 'Then Arkon will take you to where he found you. You have the Knowing to find your way back to the Humans.'

'What will I tell them?' Fenn whispered. He was trembling a little.

'You will know. But you will not know how to find your way back to us. That Knowing will pass from you. Look at me, Fenn.'

He raised his eyes. He began to feel dizzy, his head swimming. When it cleared, he couldn't tell if he'd been out of it for seconds or minutes.

'I'm sorry, what were you saying?' he asked.

The Most Ancient waved the question aside.

'Isa has a favour to ask you. Come, Isa.'

'It is this favour.' Isa's face was so earnest, Fenn had a struggle not to smile. 'When I go to live with the Keepers,' she said, 'I'd like to make the Happening of how you saved the Yeti.'

'But I didn't, not really. It wasn't just me.'

Isa put her hands on her hips. 'It is your Happening that I want to make,' she said firmly. 'Now what would you like it to be? Tell me, Fenn, Yeti Boy.'

He looked questioningly at the Most Ancient.

She nodded.

'All right then,' he said. He didn't have to think about it. His best moment was when he had stood on the top of Visigura, the star plants at his feet, looking out over the glistening snow peaks around him. His place, for that moment. Isa listened, her eyes on him, as if she was seeing into his mind to get the picture as he described it.

'I'll do it good,' she assured him, suddenly child-like again. 'Do you think Thes will let me place it next to the Happening of Shastiri?'

'It shall be so,' said the Most Ancient. 'Fenn, you will forgive that I do not come to the feast of your leave-taking, but I am still weak from the sickness.' She reached out, and Isa gave her a small bowl of water, exquisitely carved with stars. She took a few sips, then held out her hands to Fenn, the palms upwards, as if to lift his spirit.

'The time will come when Humans and Yeti meet together, but not yet,' she said.

'But it will come,' said Isa.

'Listen, and you will hear our whistling. You will know we remember you.' The Most Ancient touched his forehead. Her touch was like cool fire. 'Always, we remember you, Fenn, Yeti Boy.'

'Thank you.' It was all he could manage to say.

Then he went to tell Arkon that in three small sunarounds he was leaving the Yeti valley.

20.

Fenn and Arkon sat perched on the edge of a rock, careful to avoid the soggy damp moss. It was too cold to sit for long. The temperature had dropped. The sky was metal grey, cast over with darker clouds. Here, the winter was moving in. But not in the Yeti valley, thought Fenn. There it would be warm, each day like a perfect day in summer. He'd lost count of how many days had passed since he and Arkon had left.

Fenn put up the hood of his anorak.

On his last night, the Yeti had held a feast in his honour, with dancing around a huge fire, and fireworks too. It had gone on till late, till after moonrise. But the next morning, everyone was up to see him off. Fenn was dismayed, afraid the goodbyes would be too much, and he'd crack up and start blubbering. But it wasn't like that. The Yeti were quiet as they waved him off, and their whistlings were soothing, like he was being wrapped in silk.

Ruala and Isa had come as far as the entrance to the valley.

Ruala was very different, thought Fenn, now all the hate had gone out of her. She was sparky and lively and funny. He understood why Arkon was keen on her.

'Be safe, Yeti Boy.' Ruala kissed him on both cheeks and hugged him. Fenn hugged her back. 'You too,' he said. Then he turned to Isa. She was crying, and clung to him very tightly.

'Your going away is a horrible Happening,' she said. 'I can't find any happiness in it!'

Fenn was almost in tears himself.

'Tell you what, Isa, let's think about you making my Happening!'

Isa nodded. 'I shall be happy when I make it, Yeti Boy.'

'I'm *hugely* happy,' smiled Fenn, 'that it's Keeper Isa who's making it for me – Yeti Boy on Visigura, with the star plants!'

Isa clapped her hands in delight, and gave a whistling that echoed in his mind long after he and Arkon had left the valley.

'Arkon,' said Fenn, with a thoughtful frown.

'What it is, Yeti Boy?'

'About the star plant. Just a little plant! But it was

163

able to cure the deadly Yellow Sickness. It's amazing when you think of it. Plant Power, I suppose you could call it!' grinned Fenn.

Arkon grinned back. 'I call it, just how it is!'

'When I grow up, I think I'll study plants, all sorts, and discover how they can be used to cure things.'

'Don't Humans have this Knowing?'

'Not like the Yeti. Hey, did you see that?'

A hawk swooped up, clutching its prey.

'It looks like a mouse!' Fenn pulled a face at the victim's plight but Arkon wasn't bothered.

'It's the hawk way,' he shrugged.

Fenn thought of the snow leopard. If he had killed it, would Arkon have said, 'It's the human way'? If the snow leopard had killed him, would he have said the same thing the other way round?

They watched till the hawk was out of sight, and moved on.

The going was hard, but not as dangerous as it had been on Visigura. Occasionally they had to squeeze along ledges with sheer drops below, but Fenn wasn't as scared with Arkon leading the way.

Every now and then Arkon caused a rock-fall behind them so there was no turning back. Fenn had a try at the rock-fall whistling himself, without success, and he remembered a story in the Bible where the sounding of trumpets caused a whole city to fall. At least he'd thought it was just a story. Now, he wasn't so sure.

'Will you teach me the rock-fall whistling, Arkon?'

Arkon shook his head. 'It's enough that I do it, Yeti Boy. We do not want to bring down the whole mountain!'

As they went on, Fenn noticed that snow had already fallen higher up on the mountains.

'No wonder I'm so cold.' He blew on his fingers. 'They've gone blue,' he said. 'Which way do we go now?'

Arkon hesitated.

Fenn thought he was puzzling out the answer.

'We are here, Yeti Boy.'

Arkon pointed.

'You were standing there when you first saw me. Over there,' he pointed again, 'is where you fell.'

'But it can't be,' said Fenn. 'It just can't be!'

A few moments ago it had seemed ages since they'd left the warmth of the Yeti valley. Now it seemed no time at all.

'I'm sure it wasn't here,' he pressed. 'We've got much, much further to go.'

Then he saw the track that he'd followed up from the camp. Fenn went very white. He'd been dreading this moment. He kept hoping that somehow, something would happen, and it would never come. He hadn't thought beyond that. What would happen if the camp had packed up? But he'd survived on Visigura; he'd get by for a while. It wasn't that which was tearing him apart inside. He wanted to ask Arkon to take him back with him, to beg, and plead. But no words would come, not even a whistling.

He had some tissues somewhere. He fumbled in his anorak pocket. There was something caught in the lining. It was the saligram. He'd meant to ask the Most Ancient if he could keep it, but he'd forgotten.

'I don't want to take anything I shouldn't. Here, you'd better have it, Arkon.'

'Remember what you told me on Visigura, about the little creature and the sea? I told it all to the Most Ancient!' beamed Arkon proudly. Then he put the saligram back in Fenn's hand and wrapped Fenn's fingers over it. 'The Most Ancient says she wants you to keep it, Yeti Boy!'

Fenn's face lit up. 'But that's brilliant!'

'You have a little creature stone and so has this Yeti!' Arkon paused. 'I shall keep it for always,' he added.

'Arkon, did the Most Ancient *really* say I could take it with me?'

'Would I say if she hadn't, Yeti Boy!'

They laughed, relieved by the familiar banter. When it faded, there was silence between them.

Arkon spoke at last. His voice trembled. 'You and me will not be meeting again,' he said.

'Don't say that, Arkon.'

'I say it because it is so.' Arkon placed a hand on his heart. 'Always I remember you here, Yeti Boy. Now go, and show those Humans how to catch a fish, like I show you! You haven't forgotten the how of it?'

'Of course not! Of course I haven't. I haven't forgotten anything since you first found me, Arkon.

And I just might surprise you.' Fenn grinned shakily. 'I think I've got the Bee Sound at last. Listen to this. What's that?' he frowned, and turned quickly to look.

Fenn saw a wiry-haired dog nosing its way round the rock. Then he saw two men on horseback. They wore tunics and baggy trousers, with daggers tucked into their belts.

Fenn gave a shout of warning.

'Arkon!'

But Arkon had already gone.

Fenn knew what would come.

There it was, the rock-fall.

The men heard it too, but thought nothing of it. They circled around Fenn, peering at him suspiciously, but he wasn't looking at them.

Fenn stared at where Arkon had stood just moments before. What was it Arkon had said to him, when he was carrying him to the valley and his body was racked with pain? It wasn't just his body that was hurting now, it was all of him, right through.

Fenn smiled, a little, as Arkon's words came back to him. 'Put the hurt in a bubble. Blow it away.'

Fenn blew, his breath frosting instantly on the air.

The men drew back, and touched their heads as if he was crazy. Then they went off in a huddle and conferred between themselves. They moved in again, closer. They prodded him and his backpack. He let them take it from him. They snorted with disgust at finding nothing in it other than an empty water bottle, and were about to head off when an elderly man joined them. He was tugging the reins of a pack-horse that was laden with goodness knows what. At the sight of Fenn, his eyes lit up as if he'd found a pot of gold.

'Speak englis?' he asked.

Fenn nodded.

The elderly man talked excitedly with his companions.

'We take you,' they said. They were all smiles now.

Fenn didn't ask where they were taking him. He didn't feel he had a choice in the matter. The elderly man offered him a place on his horse. He shook his head, indicating that he would walk.

Fenn saw the camp in the distance. There seemed to be no one about. The two younger men gripped Fenn, as if afraid he might make off, and sent up a shout.

Tishaw was the first on the scene.

'Missy!' he called.

Kate came quickly from the tent that served as a laboratory.

'What's going on?' she asked.

The horsemen stood aside, and pointed.

Kate saw a tall slim boy, hair to his shoulders, his face a deep tan, with the brightest, clearest eyes.

'Fenn.'

She came towards him like a sleepwalker and reached out her hand and gently touched his arm as if testing that he was real.

Hubbert quietly approached, and stood beside her.

'Jack, it's Fenn. They've brought Fenn back.'

All three stared at each other, scarcely breathing.

Fenn couldn't sleep. The tent felt stifling. He got up and went outside. A light snow was falling. The next day, Kate had told him, they were packing up camp.

'Another day, and we'd have been gone.'

Hubbert put his arm around her. 'I told you, Katie, the luck of the Sanaskars is with you, or against you.'

'Yes,' she laughed. 'I know you did, Jack, Mr Oh-So-Clever!'

Kate wasn't as he remembered her, thought Fenn, watching the snow drifting down. She seemed quite nice in fact. She didn't barge at him with questions. He thought maybe Jack Hubbert had warned her off. But Fenn had already planned what he would say. The men who had found him had made it easier. Anticipating the reward, and hoping to get even more, they made out they'd been taking care of him for much longer than they had. Before then, Fenn volunteered, he'd lived in different places in the mountains, but it was all a bit of a blur. Kate and Jack assumed, as he intended, that he'd been found by tribesmen, like those who'd brought him back to the camp, and had been passed like a parcel from one to the other.

Jack mentioned the Yeti footprint.

'I saw a Yeti once,' he said in a way that invited Fenn to pick up on it.

'Oh, did you?' Fenn said politely, and left it at that.

Now, he walked on to the edge of the camp. He gazed up at the mountains. Somewhere in the midst of the mountains, Arkon was making his way home. In

the valley, they would be waiting for his return. Ruala, of course, Isa and the Most Ancient and Burso and Cheb. Everyone. They would be wondering about him, too.

'I must let them know I'm safe,' thought Fenn. 'I'll send a whistling. The whistling for my name – Yeti Boy!'

He cupped his hands to his mouth and gave the whistling, loud and strong. He could feel the vibration. He could still feel it as he made his way back to his tent.

Fenn unzipped the flap-door.

'I'll sleep better if I leave it open,' he thought.

When he woke the next morning, Fenn saw the winter sun was up already. The shadows were gone from the mountains. It had stopped snowing and the sky was brilliantly blue.

Fenn glanced at his watch. It was after midnight.

'That'll do for now,' he said.

He saved his work on the computer and tidied his notes to finish typing them up tomorrow. He felt a surge of excitement. For some years now, he and his research team had been working to develop a combination of plants as a cure for a fatal virus that proved resistant to synthetic chemicals. The latest tests suggested they were on the brink of a breakthrough.

He was too revved up to sleep. He'd have something to eat, he decided. He stood up, and his eyes fell on the glass case, mounted on the wall. He walked over to it, and took out the saligram. He closed his hand around it, not looking, just holding it.

At last, he turned back to his computer and set up a new file. When the morning light fell into his study, he was still writing. He didn't hear his wife, Claire, or young daughter get up.

The door opened, and they burst in.

'Fenn, you've been working all night. You should know better.'

'It's not good for you, Dad.'

'Not guilty!' he pleaded. 'I haven't been working. I've been writing about when I was in the Sanaskar Mountains.'

'Oh?' said Claire, surprised. 'You never seem to want to talk about it.'

'I know that Kate and Jack have been to the

Sanaskars, but I didn't know you had, Dad.'

'I was a few years older than you, Isa. It's all here!' Fenn tapped the pile of paper he'd printed off during the night. 'Tell you what, let's have some breakfast and I'll read it to you. What do you say?'

They broke off every now and again for a drink and a snack. It was late afternoon before Fenn put down the last page.

'I've never told anyone any of this before,' he said. 'But last night, I knew it was the time.'

Claire and Isa went up and hugged him.

'Yeti Boy!' they both laughed together.

Isa looked at the saligram. 'Maybe Arkon is looking at his little creature stone, right now!'

'And maybe,' smiled Claire, 'Keeper Isa is eating a peach from her peach tree!'

Isa went to the desk and picked up a pencil. 'I've decided I would like to be a Keeper,' she said.

Isa drew quickly, not lifting the pencil from the paper. Then she held up her drawing.

It was an all but perfect star.

'Maybe you will be a Keeper, Isa, when the time comes.' Fenn went to put the drawing on the wall, next to the saligram. He paused and looked up, out through the window.

'What is it?' they asked.

'Listen,' said Fenn, softly.

He heard it often, a whistling that could have been the song of a bird, but Fenn knew that it was not.

THE DREAM SNATCHER
by Kara May

Jodie knows that her dreams are special. So when the rest of the people in the town sell their dreams to the mysterious Dream Snatcher, they become rich while Jodie stays poor. But they are only rich with material things... without their dreams they cannot sleep. And without their sleep they cannot enjoy their new lives. It is only Jodie who can save the town when the Dream Snatcher threatens to destroy it!

*Another Collins Red Storybook
to add to your collection!*

Collins
An Imprint of HarperCollins*Publishers*
www.fireandwater.com

Order Form

To order direct from the publishers, just make a list of the titles you want and fill in the form below:

Name ....

Address ....

....

....

Send to: Dept 6, HarperCollins Publishers Ltd, Westerhill Road, Bishopbriggs, Glasgow G64 2QT.

Please enclose a cheque or postal order to the value of the cover price, plus:

UK & BFPO: Add £1.00 for the first book, and 25p per copy for each additional book ordered.

Overseas and Eire: Add £2.95 service charge. Books will be sent by surface mail but quotes for airmail despatch will be given on request.

A 24-hour telephone ordering service is available to holders of Visa, MasterCard, Amex or Switch cards on 0141- 772 2281.

Collins
An *Imprint* of HarperCollins*Publishers*